MICHAEL
MARTONE

MICHAEL
MARTONE
by
MICHAEL
MARTONE

FC2

NORMAL/TALLAHASSEE

Published by FC2 with support provided by Florida State University, the Publications Unit of the Department of English at Illinois State University, and the Florida Arts Council of the Florida Division of Cultural Affairs. This project is supported in part also by an award from the National Endowment for the Arts, which believes that a great nation deserves great art.

Address all inquiries to: Fiction Collective Two, Florida State University, c/o English Department, Tallahassee, FL 32306-1580

ISBN: Paper, 1-57366-126-0

Library of Congress Cataloging-in-Publication Data
Martone, Michael.
  Michael Martone / by Michael Martone.— 1st ed.
    p. cm.
  ISBN 1-57366-126-0
  1. Autobiographical fiction, American. 2. Fort Wayne (Ind.)—Fiction. 3. Humorous stories, American. 4. Authorship—Fiction. 5. Authors—Fiction. I. Title.
  PS3563.A7414M53 2005
  813'.54—dc22
                                        2005020391

Cover Design: Lou Robinson
Book Design: Tara Reeser

Produced and printed in the United States of America
Printed on recycled paper with soy ink

NATIONAL
ENDOWMENT
FOR THE ARTS

Michael Martone thanks the editors of the following journals for publishing parts of *Michael Martone* in their magazines and for considering to do so in the contributors' notes sections and nowhere else: the *Journal*, *Gulf Coast*, *Flyway*, *Epoch*, *Willow Springs*, *Northwest Review*, *Lake Effect*, *Western Humanities Review*, *Ninth Letter*, *Brooklyn Rail*, *Little Engines*, *Water-Stone Review*, the *Literary Review*, *Indiana Review*, *Hunger Mountain*, *Hayden's Ferry*, *Sou'wester*, *Denver Quarterly*, *Crazyhorse*, *McSweeney's*, *Passages North*, *New Orleans Review*, *Gargoyle*, *Parakeet*, *Idaho Review*, *Yalobusha Review*, and *Web del Sol*. Michael Martone thanks team FC2: R.M. Berry, Brenda Mills, Lance Olsen, Cris Mazza, Tara Reeser, Ali Salerno, and Lou Robinson and Zachary Martin, both with Hoosier roots. Michael Martone thanks Sandy Huss, Wendy Rawling, Robin Behn, Joel Brouwer, Joyelle McSweeney, Patti White, and all Michael Martone's colleagues and students at Bama. Michael Martone thanks the following names: Michael Martone, Susan Neville, Michael J. Rosen, Michael Wilkerson, Robin Hemley, Rikki Ducornet, Ann Jones, Melanie Rae Thon, Nancy Esposito, Paul Maliszewski, Karen Brennan, John Barth, Kathy Hall, and Valerie Berry, physician attending. Michael Martone thanks all the patient recipients of all the postcards and those who answer same with same. Blessed be general delivery. Michael Martone thanks Marian Young for standing by. Michael Martone thanks Sam and Nick for being Sam and Nick. Michael Martone thanks Theresa Pappas, who calls Michael Martone by Michael Martone's real name.

For Mother and Father, co-contributors

TABLE OF CONTENTS

CONTRIBUTOR'S NOTE

Michael Martone was born in Fort Wayne, Indiana, and was educated in the public schools there. His first published work, a poem titled "Recharging Time," and a character sketch, "Tim, the Experience," about his brother, appeared in the *Forum*, an annual literary magazine produced by the school system featuring contributions from its students. His mother, a high school freshman English teacher at the time, in fact, wrote the poem and the character sketch, signing her son's name to the work and sending it to the editor, another English teacher at a south side junior high school who had been a sorority sister, Kappa Alpha Theta, in college. Indeed, most of his papers written for school were written by his mother. Examples included English research papers, history term papers, translations from the Latin, speeches, and lab reports. It began innocently enough with his mother writing his essays, the prose supposedly dictated by the son to his mother, whose penmanship was far and away more legible. This arrangement, her son sitting across the kitchen table, in a sense thinking out loud as she transcribed his thoughts with the same pen she used to grade her own students' papers, engendered in her a very active editorial intervention, which began to shape the spontaneous utterances emanating from her son. Soon this situation evolved to the point where her son, sat silently while she wrote an original response to his initial prompt. Once she finished the first draft, she read it back to her son, who made a few minor suggestions as to form, style, and content. It was at this time and under these conditions that Martone began thinking of himself as a writer. His mother promoted that view in other ways, announcing to her friends at the local chapter of the educational honorary that her son had an aptitude for writing. The collaboration continued through college, where assignments were mailed home and returned or, in some extreme cases, the prose response was communicated via the telephone and copied out in a rather cramped and illegible longhand in the dormitory phone booth. Most of Martone's first book of stories and his occasional essays on the subject of writing, published under his own name, were written by his mother, who learned, finally, to type in 1979, the year she wrote his graduate thesis. Today Martone receives microcassette recordings his mother has made of his future work with the hard copy arriving by fax or courier and little or no interaction between the collaborators prior to the work's appearance. Martone is hard-pressed to tell you what exactly of his published work could truly be said to be his original contribution, if any, including this contributor's note and the contribution published somewhere else in this volume.

Contributor's Note

Michael Martone was born at St. Joseph's Hospital in Fort Wayne, Indiana, in 1955. It is interesting to note that the attending physician was a Doctor Frank Burns, Major, United States Army, retired, and recently returned to Fort Wayne following service in the police action in Korea. It was the same Dr. Burns, it turned out, who years later served as the model for the character "Frank Burns" appearing in the novel *M*A*S*H* authored by Richard Hooker, and in the movie and television versions based on the book. Martone recalls the modest premiere of the Altman film in 1970 and its initial screening at the Embassy Theater in downtown Fort Wayne. Dr. Burns, who had continued, after Martone's birth (it had been a difficult one, sunny-side up, where forceps were used), to be his mother's gynecologist, arrived at the theater, the guest of honor, in a 1959 Cadillac Seville provided by Means Motor Company on Main Street. Sally Kellerman and Jo Ann Pflug also were there. All during the run of the television series,

Dr. Burns, now in semiretirement, happily appeared at strip-mall ribbon cuttings and restaurant openings, a kind of official goodwill ambassador, and took the ribbing from the public whose perception of his character had been derived from what they had read or seen in the movies and on television. His son, Frank Jr., was two years ahead of Martone at North Side High School. Frank Jr. anchored the 4x440 relay for the Redskin varsity track and field club, where Martone served as team manager. Martone remembers Dr. Burns, team physician, coaching him in the use of analgesic balm and the scrubbing of cinders out from beneath the skin after a runner fell on the track. It was Dr. Burns who, later, diagnosed Martone's mother's ovarian cancer in 1979 and performed the failed hysterectomy that led to his mother's death that summer. It was Dr. Burns, still in his surgical scrubs, who met the family in the waiting room of St. Joseph Hospital in Fort Wayne, the same hospital where Martone, twenty-four years before, had been born, delivered, by means of forceps, by Dr. Burns. The television was on, of course, an RCA model made in Bloomington, Indiana, and Martone remembers how hard it was not to watch it while, in a strange way, he also felt that he was watching himself listening to Dr. Burns rehearse the final few minutes of his, Martone's, mother's life.

CONTRIBUTOR'S NOTE

Michael Martone was born in Fort Wayne, Indiana, and grew up there. His father, Antonio Martone, who worked as a motorman on the streetcars of Naples, silenced the sounded "e" on the end of his name upon entering the United States. In New York, Antonio Martone boarded the Pennsylvania Railroad westbound only to detrain a few stops early, in Fort Wayne, thinking he had arrived in Chicago. In Fort Wayne he stayed, married, and raised a family. He would often tell his son of the singularity of their shared last name. Antonio Martone liked to take Michael Martone to the Allen County Library and there have his son pick a phone book, any phone book, from the collection of directories in the reference section to see whether he could find another Martone. Martone does not remember ever finding another Martone in the phone books of distant cities. His father said, "See, I told you" after each attempt, and then they would go once again to look at the photo archive of rolling stock and steam locomotives built by the

15

shops in Fort Wayne during the early part of the century. It wasn't until Martone moved to Baltimore to attend graduate school that he discovered another Martone. Walking out of the Lexington Market on Eutaw Street, finishing a cup of root beer brewed by the Amish, Martone discovered an advertisement for Martone's Cleaners painted on the third-story brick wall of a nearby building. His peeling name curled around a faded image of a rabbit being pulled out of a top hat by its ears. He spent some time walking the surrounding neighborhood, trying to find Martone's Cleaners, but found nothing save the boarded-up storefronts, several wig shops, a snowball stand, and a stable where some Arabbers kept their ponies. It wasn't until much later, when he lived in Iowa, that he actually found someone else with his last name. In Iowa he applied, for the first time, to the NEA for a fellowship in fiction writing. Martone opened a letter from the agency rejecting his application. "We are sorry," it began. In conclusion, the letter promised to return his slides under separate cover. This was curious, since Martone had applied in writing, not in any fine art category. He called the office in Washington. After some searching, the secretary told him that there seemed to be another Michael Martone, a photographer, who lived in New York City. Michael Martone asked for the other Michael Martone's address so he could send him the slides when they arrived under separate cover. When they appeared, Martone opened the package and looked at the slides, holding them up to the window. The pictures were strange and beautiful, double and triple exposures of mannequins and antique cameras arranged into collages of ghostly layers. Martone sent the slides back to the other Martone in New York with a letter introducing himself and explaining what happened. He said he was sorry that the photographs had not been awarded a fellowship and told him about his father, who said how rare the name Martone was. A few weeks later Martone received a letter from Michael Martone, who was quite excited about the coincidence and asked detailed questions about his, Martone's, family history. Michael Martone also wrote that his father had always told him there were no other Martones. They stayed in touch. Martone once visited Martone's East 15th Street apartment, a warren of shelves stacked with old plates and prints and the collection of cameras and plastic body parts. They talked about one day doing a collaboration of text and pictures, but it never worked out. Martone asked him whether he, in his research, had ever come across Martone's Cleaners, and he showed him a photograph of the wall advertisement taken from the same angle Martone remembered from seeing the sign for the first time. Martone told Martone of his hospitalization and gave him a copy of his book, *Dark Light*, which now, years later, appears as one of Martone's titles if you do an author search on Amazon.com. Doing an electronic search today, Martone has discovered many other Michael Martones. One is a judge in Michigan who is famous for his innovative sentences. Once he made a man convicted of disturbing the peace with rock and roll music listen to Montovani nonstop for hours at a time. Another Michael Martone is a very funny writer who lives in Chicago and contributes regularly to the *Modern Humorist*. Michael Martone's pictures are often compared to those of Diane Arbus: grotesques, especially the self-portraits, that Michael Martone, the one whose contributor's note this is, finds disturbing in more ways than one. Martone gave Martone one of those self-portraits. In it, Martone wears a porkpie hat, his head turned in profile, and the face of an old viewfinder Leica camera bleeds through Martone's startled expression. Back in Iowa, Martone framed that photograph and gradually fell out of touch with Martone, the exchange of genealogies and individual life stories complete. Later still, Martone moved to Cambridge, Massachusetts, and on his arrival in town someone, during an introduction, said she was surprised to learn that he was a photographer too. It turned out that the other Michael Martone, the photographer, had an exhibit at the Fogg that week but Martone hadn't known it. He took his skeptical father, who was in town to help him move east but also to ride the T's Green Line streetcars, to the Fogg to meet another Martone. Together they looked at the display of photographs and saw together, too, the famous self-portrait of Vincent Van Gogh. On the steps of the museum, Martone's father took a snapshot of his son and the other Michael Martone while that Michael Martone took a picture of Martone's father taking the picture of the two Michael Martones.

CONTRIBUTOR'S NOTE

Michael Martone was born in Fort Wayne, Indiana, and grew up there. Currently, he lives in Tuscaloosa, Alabama, where he teaches at the university. Martone hadn't remembered, when he took the job in Tuscaloosa, that he had ever visited the city before he came for his initial interview. As a child growing up in Indiana, he traveled every spring, vacationing with his family. His mother was a teacher, so the family got away during the school breaks each spring, driving on long road-trips to distant final destinations where they would stay a day or two at the most before turning around and heading back to Indiana. On these trips Martone took his baseball mitt and several scuffed balls. When they stopped for lunch or dinner, and before getting in the car in the morning, and before going into the motel room at night, he played catch with his father in the parking lots. Many of these trips led south to the spring training camps of professional baseball teams in Florida, where, before the games, he played catch with his father in the parking lots of the stadiums. On these trips his mother filmed the occasions with a boxy Kodak Super 8 movie camera. There always seemed to be plenty of light, in contrast to the sunless winters of his boyhood home in Indiana. The home movies she developed of these trips consisted mainly of the recording of these games of catch. Martone would watch himself wind up, pretending to pitch in parking lots outside Mammoth Cave or on top of Lookout Mountain by the gates of Rock City. The camera recorded every throw, every toss of every session, pausing on Martone or his father and then frantically following the ball, a blur, back and forth. The scene was often punctuated by Martone's father hurling the ball up into the air to simulate a high pop fly. His mother would catch the ball hanging in the air for what seemed like seconds, a buff speck on the blue sky, and then follow its descent into Martone's freshly oiled (he took Neet's Foot Oil with him on these trips) glove. Their neighbors were always slightly confused by these movies and his mother's narration. "I think this was a McDonald's in Knoxville," she said. "This is the Florida Welcome Center." The throwing and the catching went on for five, ten minutes. Often an entire film cassette would be expended capturing the game. When the ball got past one or the other of the subjects, his mother followed it as it skipped along the asphalt at the parking lot's edge, where she would hold the shot, while the ball was being retrieved, on a scrawny palm tree, a frantic mockingbird, or a man putting gas in a pickup truck. Recently, Martone received a videotape compilation of these movies. His mother had transferred them to the tape, splicing all the trips into one long trip and adding a jazzy musical soundtrack to the mix. On the phone she told her son to pay particular attention to the sequence that begins in the parking lot of the Cyclorama in Atlanta and ends in the French Quarter of New Orleans. There are several restaurant and motel parking lots in between, but she was, she said, quite convinced that one of them

20

was filmed in Tuscaloosa. Perhaps, she said, the one after breakfast or the one after lunch. She was amazed by the coincidence—that as a child of twelve her son left this evidence of his first visit to the place where he now resides. Martone, for his part, sits in the darkened TV room of his comfortable three-bedroom ranch house in Tuscaloosa and runs the tape back and forth, back and forth, replaying each pitch and catch. He marvels at the energy he had as a child, likes the almost natural way he seems to pitch and catch. He has not thrown a baseball in years, does not remember the last time he did so. He tries to see in the background of each shot some clue, some solid glimpse of evidence, that this really was Tuscaloosa then. If he could find such a hint, he suspects, he would drive out to that very location, a place not that far away, and gather in the fresh intelligence of the spot he inhabited for a few minutes during a part of one spring years ago.

Contributor's Note

M ichael Martone was born in Fort Wayne, Indiana, and he was educated in the public schools there. He attended Indiana University in Bloomington, where, during freshman orientation, he took part in the famous Kinsey Report by completing a survey of his sexual history. Alfred Kinsey, a biology professor at the university, had begun his famous work on human sexual response when he was teaching, after the war, the "marriage" course, an early attempt in the health curriculum to provide information in what was called then sexual hygiene. One day, a coed who was to be married that summer approached Kinsey after a lecture to ask what she could expect from her husband, and Kinsey, always the scientist, couldn't answer her because he didn't have, he realized, any hard scientific evidence. "I'll get back to you," he told her, and began his decades-long project of collecting oral interviews, written personal narratives, taped anecdotal commentary, and computer-scanned surveys from a vast range of informants in order to build a workable database of sexual behavior. There, years later, in a crowded lecture room in Ballantine Hall, Michael Martone participated in the very same ongoing effort of data gathering, carefully blackening with the provided No. 2 pencil the appropriate bubble corresponding to the numbered response most accurately representing such desired information as his masturbatory habits and history, his sexual preference, his preferred positions (there were illustrations), and the time, to the nearest minute, of his recovery after "performing vigorous coitus." The room fell silent as the freshman class bent to this initial collegian task required of them, the quiet broken only by the scratching of pencil lead on the rigid manila IBM cards and the counterpunctual response of the rubbing of rubber erasers. Afterward, Martone remembers racing from the building into a bright fall day, the trees of Dunn Meadow just taking on the color of the season. That night, he called his mother, who had also been a student at Indiana University, to ask her whether she, too, had been recruited to contribute to Professor Kinsey's report, indicating to her, as best he could, the extent and duration of the statistical instrument he had just endured. "No," his mother responded, "they didn't have that when I was there. I did take this facts-of-life course the spring before I married Daddy." She went on to say that she didn't learn much, that the class had been dry and very statistical in nature. "I even asked the professor about it." It hadn't mattered, she concluded, since shortly after that meeting with the professor who had told her he would get back to her about her questions, she and her soon-to-be husband figured out how to go about the very thing that had been so mysterious. Late one night, in a classroom where, in his senior year at Indiana University, Martone would take a class on Chaucer, his parents, ignorant of contraception in spite of the courses they took, managed to conceive their son. When asked, years later, by her son for further details, his mother simply said she couldn't recall much more about that night but that she could make something up if that would help.

CONTRIBUTOR'S NOTE

M ichael Martone was born in Fort Wayne, Indiana, and grew up there, leaving, at seventeen, to work as a roustabout in the last traveling circus to winter in the state. He has held many jobs since then, including night auditor in a resort hotel, stenographer for the National Labor Relations Board, and clerk for a regional bookstore chain run by associates of the Gambino crime family. For the last twenty years Martone has been digging ditches. As a ditchdigger, he has helped lay agricultural tiling, both original fired-clay tile and flexible PVC tubing, in the farm fields of northern Indiana, Ohio, and southern Michigan. He worked on the national project that buried thousands of miles of fiber-optic cable along active and abandoned right-of-ways of North American railroads. He has often contracted to do the initial excavations at archaeological digs throughout the Midwest's extensive network of mounds, built by archaic pre-Columbian civilizations, where he would roughly remove the initial unremarkable strata for the scholars who followed at the site with hand trowels and dental instruments. Often when digging ditches, Martone would employ a poacher's spade made in the United Kingdom by the Bulldog Company and given to him by the Nobel Prize-winning Irish poet Seamus Heaney, who ordered it from the Smith & Hawken catalog and gave it to Martone as a going-away present when Martone left Boston, where he had been digging clams. Its ash, "Y"-shaped handle still retains a remnant of the ribbon that decorated the gift. Martone has operated a backhoe, constructing drainage ditches, and he has used a Ditch Witch when digging a trench for buried electrical conduit in housing developments around Las Vegas, Nevada. He has been certified to run a dragline as well as licensed to maintain boilers in obsolete steam shovels. He is proficient at foundation work, having been employed for four years in the area of poured form and precast concrete retaining walls and building footings. Briefly, he worked as a sandhog, tunneling a new PATH tube between Manhattan and New Jersey. Martone has mined coal and gypsum in Kentucky and repaired the sewers of Paris and Vienna. Honorably discharged from the Seabees, he once helped fortify, through the entrenchment and the construction of sand berms and tank traps, the Saudi Arabian city of Qarr during the Gulf War. He has buried culvert in Nova Scotia and created leech fields and septic systems in Stewartstown, Pennsylvania. Having installed irrigations systems on the Trent Jones-designed golf courses of Alabama, Martone recently took a position as a gravedigger at the Roman Catholic Cemetery in his hometown in order to be closer to his family. Using the newly purchased Komatsu excavator, he recently dug the grave for his mother, who died unexpectedly in her sleep. He observed the funeral from the cab of the machine, waiting until the mourners had departed to remove the Astroturf blanket covering the spoil and then back-filling the opening and replacing the squares of real turf on the dirt. Since

28

that time, on his days off, Martone digs, with the poacher's spade given to him by the Nobel Prize-winning Irish poet Seamus Heaney, his own grave, or at least attempts to dig his own grave. All of these efforts, so far, have been filled back in, since the resulting holes, to his professional eye, were never quite right.

CONTRIBUTOR'S NOTE

Michael Martone, born in Fort Wayne, Indiana, published his first book, *Big Words*, in graduate school. The children's book could use only thirty age-appropriate words taken from the Dolch Word List.

CONTRIBUTOR'S NOTE

Michael Martone was born and raised in Fort Wayne, Indiana. His mother died shortly after his birth of complications arising from a difficult pregnancy and delivery. Every year on his birthday, Martone's father would tell his son the story of his birth and of the death of his mother. In telling the story, his father remembered the moment when his wife, waking up after the long, difficult labor, asked him, "We lost the baby?" "No," his father said he said to her, "No, we didn't lose the baby." His father told the story so many times that his son, while growing up, came to believe that it was his earliest memory. He remembered his mother propped up in her hospital bed, his father at the other end, his head down on the blue wool blanket. Her eyes fluttering open. "We lost the baby?" "No, we didn't," his father answers. Not much later, she dies. He didn't remember that. And he remembered, for a while, all the times his father, collapsed in the rubble of wrapping paper or slumped at the kitchen table brushing cake crumbs onto a napkin or picking candle wax from the tablecloth or sitting at the end of his bed in his dark bedroom, telling the story, the first and last words of his mother, both a statement and a question. Martone, who is himself a father, remembered again the story of his own birth and all its annual retellings while he sat in a surgical recovery room waiting for his son to be born. He had been told to wait there when his wife was wheeled into the surgery for an emergency C-section. There had been no time for him to scrub up, and a nurse at the head of the gurney had pointed him into the recovery room as they raced on. "Wait here," she said. In the recovery room there were a dozen laboring women (it had been a very busy night and there was no other place to induce). In beds, all of them were attached to chemical drips inducing their contractions, amplified and sped up by the synthetic hormone Pitocin. He sat on a stool by the door and watched as the spasms of pain gripped first one, then the next woman and the next woman until, it seemed, all were in various stages of writhing, gulping for air, clutching the sheets. The monitors they were hooked up to spat out ribbons of paper. The numbers on the screens pulsed and lowered in value as women emerged from the most recent contraction. As each woman returned from her contraction, she opened her eyes and focused on him waiting by the door until all the women were staring his way. At that moment he remembered his own mother coming to consciousness on the day of his birth and on each of his subsequent childhood birthdays. The women were not happy to see him there by the door. He decided, then, to take a walk, and he wandered through the hospital corridors. In every room on the floor another woman was in some kind of labor. There were howls, urgent murmuring, hoarse breathing, mumbles, commands for pushing. In the hallway and in the lounges other women at the beginning of labor waited uncomfortably for a room. It was a big city hospital. It was long ago. But, after a while, he made his way back through the corridors and lobbies and found the nurse, who had been looking for him, who told him his wife and son had been taken upstairs, where he found them, finally, both asleep. He sat in a plastic chair pulled up to the end of the bed, told himself to remember everything, and waited for one or the other or both to wake up and ask him what had happened.

CONTRIBUTOR'S NOTE

Michael Martone was born in Fort Wayne, Indiana, and grew up there, attending the public schools. He went to Butler University in Indianapolis, where, because his mother was an alumna, he received, as a legacy, a reduction of his tuition. Growing up in Fort Wayne, he would travel with his mother each fall to Indianapolis to participate in the homecoming festivities that the college staged. One year, Peter Lupus, who was then starring in the television series *Mission: Impossible*, was the grand marshall of the parade. Mr. Lupus had grown up in Indianapolis, and his family ran a Greek restaurant in Chinatown on the city's near south side. Martone's mother had been a sorority sister with Mr. Lupus's sister, Helen, and his mother had been pinned to Mr. Lupus for a while during her sophomore year, when he was a senior. Martone knew this because his mother would mention it every time they watched the television show together. "There's Peter Lupus," she would say and tell him about how they met in an acting class. Peter

Lupus played the muscle in the band of secret operatives depicted in the television series. *Mission: Impossible* was a show about spies putting on performances that would deceive and entrap foreign dictators one week and international criminals the next. Martone enjoyed the moment at the end of the show when the actors playing actors removed their spongy, latex lifelike masks at the end of the mission. Often, Mr. Lupus removed his shirt as well. Martone's mother believes that he now owns a chain of health clubs in Sarasota, but when they met again at the brunch held in a striped tent in Holcomb Gardens during Butler's homecoming, he was still filming episodes of *Mission: Impossible* in California. Mr. Lupus told young Martone then that the masks were not really that lifelike. Other actors actually played the characters who had different faces. Mr. Lupus and the other actors were filmed taking off rather featureless rubber masks in such a way that it looked like they were taking off the actual other faces. While in college, his mother and Mr. Lupus had been in a play together, Shakespeare's *A Midsummer Night's Dream*, performed right there in the gardens where they were now eating brunch. His mother had been Titania and Mr. Lupus had been one of the rustic players, not Bottom, but the one who played Thisbe in the play. He wished that he had been Bottom, he said to Martone's mother. They talked for a long time after that while Martone sat at the table with them and most of the crowd moved on up to the campus for the bed races and the judging of the mascot bulldogs. The football game would start soon in the Butler Bowl next to the Hinkle Fieldhouse. Martone attended three homecomings when he was a student at the university, but in his senior year, for a host of reasons, he left and graduated eventually from Indiana University in Bloomington. While he was at Butler, his mother loved to visit him on campus and did so often. Martone saw Peter Lupus one other time in person shortly after the homecoming. His mother woke him one night near Christmas when his father was working second shift at the telephone company. She took him downstairs, and there in the living room was Peter Lupus. "Peter is helping me move furniture," his mother told him. And just then, Mr. Lupus squatted deep at the knees and lifted the television cabinet and walked it to the other side of the room before setting it down under the big window. Then Martone's mother told Mr. Lupus to move it a little farther to the right, and he did.

Contributor's Note

Michael Martone was born in Fort Wayne, Indiana, where he worked every summer, while attending high school and college the rest of the year, for International Harvester on the assembly line at the company's truck plant on the city's east end. Then, before the company went bankrupt and they subsequently closed the plant and moved what jobs were left to a factory in Missouri, International Harvester had been one of the largest employers in the city. No one called it International Harvester, however, saying instead that you worked at International or, more likely, at the Harvester. Martone preferred the latter, liked the *the* added to the single name. People in Fort Wayne worked for *the* Harvester or *the* GE or for *the* Pennsy, the railroad that ran from New York and Philadelphia right through Fort Wayne, close to the Harvester, then on to Chicago. And on the weekends or in the summer the people of Fort Wayne went to The Lake. The lake they would go to would be one of a hundred named lakes (James, George, Clear,

Long, Crooked, Sylvan, Wawasee) in northeastern Indiana that were all called The Lake by the people of Fort Wayne who went to them or who stayed in town and only talked about going. Martone did not go to The Lake those summers he worked at the Harvester. He was hired to cover for the permanent employees who were on their annual two-week vacations at The Lake. The plant made the TriStar truck, a cab-over semitractor that had a forward chrome grill that cut straight down from the big windshield, a flat face, a wall of metal and glass. Many of the units rolled out of the factory and right over to North American Van Lines, whose world headquarters was right next door. Martone didn't work on that line, but he couldn't help but notice the huge hulks as they were assembled. He liked the way the crew compartment, the whole big cab, was flipped forward to expose the engine buried beneath the seats. Martone worked on the Scout line. The Scout was a little closed truck that looked a lot like an army jeep and was one of the first attempts the industry made at making what later would be called the SUV. Martone is not and was not then a skilled laborer. He wasn't assigned to handle the pneumatic socket wrenches that bolted parts together nor able to operate the spot-welding torches that fused the body to the chassis nor even permitted to mask the car with paper and tape for its spray painting. Martone waited at the end of the line after the final assembly near the big doors where the finished product left the works and was driven out to the vast parking lot to wait for loading onto train cars or auto haulers pulled by TriStars. He was in quality control. He had a clipboard and even a white coat he didn't wear in the summer heat. He had a whole list of things he needed to test on every brand new Scout that nosed toward him. At this point the cars were chained to the slow-moving cable under the floor, their wheels guided by tracks. As each unit crept by, Martone had to perform a series of checks. He opened and closed the door on the driver's side; he opened the door again and got in; he adjusted the seat forward and back, back and forward; leaving the transmission in neutral, he started the engine; he locked and unlocked the door; he turned the lights on and off; he turned the windshield wipers on and off; he turned the turn indicators on and off, first the left and then the right; he tapped the horn twice; he turned off the car, leaving the key in the ignition; he hopped out, closing the door solidly behind him. Martone did this ritual eight hours a day, six days a week, all through the summer. When the whistle blew at the end of his shift (there was an actual steam whistle), Martone made his way to the locker room, where he put his clipboard and his white coat into his locker and got his lunch pail. As he stood in line waiting to punch out, Martone told himself, "Don't do it. Don't do it." He took a step up and the man at the head of the line inserted his time card. "Don't do it." Another punch and another step forward, all the time reminding himself not to do what he knew he would do. Finally, Martone punched out and he made his way to his own car through the enormous field of finished TriStars and Scouts in precise ranks and then on to the employees' lot, where many of the workers drove to work in Scouts that they had purchased right at the factory door. All the way to his car (it was his mother's car, actually, a red International Harvester Scout), Martone kept reminding himself not to do what he knew he would do. Martone waded through the sea of cars, emerged at last next to his, his mother's, own. And there, he couldn't help himself. He opened and closed the door on the driver's side; he opened the door again and got in; he adjusted the seat forward and back, back and forward; leaving the transmission in neutral, he started the engine; he locked and unlocked the door; he turned the lights on and off; he turned the windshield wipers on and off; he turned the turn indicators on and off, first the left and then the right; he tapped the horn twice; he turned off the car, leaving the key in the ignition; he hopped out, closing the door solidly behind him. He had been inside his car for a moment but now he found himself standing outside it once again. Martone always feared this moment most of all. He was afraid that once he tried to get into his car again that what had happened would happen again and he would be outside of the car at the end of it and never able to break the habit of his inspection. But he did, of course, eventually, and made his way home along the streets of Fort Wayne in a car that had been built there, where he had been born, and where, he thought then, he would never be able to leave.

Contributor's Note

Michael Martone was born in Fort Wayne, Indiana, in 1955. He taught at Harvard University, where he was the Briggs-Copeland Lecturer on Fiction after teaching for seven years at Iowa State University in Ames. Martone noticed the difference between the two schools right away. On the first day of fiction writing class, he asked his new students to introduce themselves, including in their introduction details about their class standing, their academic interests, their preferences in what they read. He also wanted to ask them where they were from. He was curious, having just come from Ames to Cambridge. "Where are you from?" he asked the first student. The student answered that he was from Lowell House. Martone, expecting an answer like Illinois or Indianapolis, didn't know what to say in response, so he nodded his head and smiled in a manner he hoped conveyed that he did in fact understand and even approved. He asked the same question of the second student, who answered without hesitating that she was from Adams House. After several more students answered in the same way, volunteering that they were from this or that house, Martone figured out they were talking about their dormitories. It also occurred to him that he was meant to understand that knowing the particular house was to also know a great deal about the one who was from there, one's tastes and preferences. It was a code that took him most of the first semester to begin to decipher, but he did finally figure out which house was preferred by athletes, for instance, or actors and musicians or those students who had a scientific bent. The rest of the first class was a disaster. Martone lectured to a restless and hostile room. He kept going while he tried to figure out what was so wrong. His students in Iowa had responded to his broad-ranging improvisations and his manner of peppering his talks with arcane trivia and personal anecdote. At Harvard, this appeared not to be working. The students sulked in their seats or stared blankly out the window. Suddenly, Martone realized that he was talking. That is to say that the fact that he was lecturing was what was wrong with the lecture. He had grown used to the natural shyness and silence of his students in Iowa. At Harvard his new students were not handicapped in the same way. They could not wait to speak, were more than prepared to do so, and once Martone realized this and allowed the students to speak, the initial discomfort disappeared at once. During the remaining five years of his tenure there, Martone barely uttered a few words each class session. In retrospect, he believes he was adored by his charges, winning teaching prizes each term and receiving excellent assessments in the student evaluations. He lived off Central Square, within walking distance of Harvard Square and 34 Kirkland, his office building at the university. Walking to work, he would pass several stores that specialized in selling used tuxedos. Martone found it curious the number of such establishments. Formal wear for him had always been acquired from a rental store, the racks and racks of suits somewhere in the back out of sight of the showroom. Mentioning it in class one day, Martone learned from his students about the "battle tuxes" that were part of their wardrobe—cheap formal party dress that could suffer the excesses of the students' celebrations, a spontaneous dive into a nearby pool, for instance. Martone ended up buying several battle tuxes for himself. To the one commencement he attended he wore a dinner jacket designed by Bill Blass, who was from Martone's hometown of Fort Wayne, Indiana. Martone took to dressing in a tux for the first day of his classes. He had inherited a blue paisley tie and cummerbund from his Uncle Wayne, which lent a jaunty and ironic flavor to the getup. In one of the last first classes, during the introductions when the students shared what houses they were from, a young woman asked him whether Sallie Gouverneur was his agent. This surprised Martone, since he never talked about his business with his students. How would any of them know who his literary agent was? It turned out that this student had interned for Sallie, who was a graduate of Radcliffe herself, and this intern had seen and sent out Martone's stories the previous summer with cover letters she had composed herself. Another student in the same class reported that she had interned in the summer at the *Atlantic Monthly*, where she received from her fellow student Martone's manuscripts, sent to the magazine to be considered. Martone remained silent as his students talked a while about the business of writing and publishing, trying to recall just which of his stories he had sent to Sallie that summer. The next year Martone took a job teaching in the creative-writing program at Syracuse University. He moved from the Boston area, heading north with a box of several tuxedoes that he never had the occasion to wear again.

CONTRIBUTOR'S NOTE

Michael Martone was born in Fort Wayne, Indiana, and was educated in the public schools there. While in fourth grade, during recess at Francis Price Elementary, Martone bit through the right half of his tongue. He had fallen while he ran across the playground. He always clenched his tongue between his teeth when he played or concentrated on his schoolwork. While reading, he bit his tongue. That day, he was being chased by Ann Jones in a game where they pretended that they were airplanes in an aerial dogfight. He tripped on an exposed tree root of the flowering crab near the four-square court. His mouth filled with blood, and he spit out a chunk of tongue into his hand. The tongue couldn't be stitched, of course, but healed quickly, forming a ragged scar, a tiny flap of which he finds he can still rub against his back teeth. That same year, he was whittling a stick in his backyard with the folding pocketknife his Grandpa Shaker gave him when he taught Martone to whittle when, in one long stoke, the blade slid through the sliver of bark on the stick and sliced into the skin of his left index finger. Today there is still a half-moon scar on that knuckle. A few months later, Martone put his right hand through a kitchen window while pounding on it in response to Stevie Leon outside messing around with his, Martone's, bike (a red, 24-inch Schwinn Typhoon). That scar runs in a zigzag line from the base of the little finger along the heel of the hand almost to the wrist. In high school Martone developed Osgood-Schlatter syndrome, which left bumps beneath both his kneecaps, indications of the calcium building up to keep the slower-growing tendons attached to the spurting growth of underlying bone. Playing football, Martone broke his right thumb in two places when cutting through the line. He was a fullback, and the accident happened during the high school football jamboree. As he sidestepped a tackle, his hand flew into the face-guard on the helmet of the pursuing linebacker. After that injury Martone wore a plaster cast that allowed him to continue practicing but prevented him from playing in any more games—the regulations stating that the heavy cast would give a player unfair advantage, the dressing used as a club on the soft tissue of his opponents. Along with the autographs and the inspirational sayings that his friends and family affixed to the cast, Martone wrote several poems and beginnings of stories, including one that was a list of his injuries and the resulting scars. Martone taught himself to write with his unencumbered left hand. He used cheap Bic pens and became adept at matching his new shaky script with the contours of the cast. The thumb took months to heal, and the cast, completely inscribed with messages, would disintegrate regularly, battered by rough contact into crumbs of plaster adhering to the grungy gauze netting. He went back to the doctors several times to have a new cast made, the old one sawn off and thrown away. When the bone finally healed, the knitting at the breaks left the knuckles there thicker than those on the other thumb while the rest of the hand, atrophied, had shriveled, the skin pale and pasty. Martone continues to use his left hand when he writes with a pen or pencil, while with all other activities requiring handedness, such as brushing his teeth or combing his hair, his right one regained its dominance. Martone has a reoccurring plantar wart on the ball of his left foot that has created a cavity the width of a few centimeters, a result of repeated procedures to remove it. He has four prominent moles or beauty marks on his face, two staggered on either side of his nose. The lower one on the left side produces one thin but very black hair that Martone shaves or plucks periodically because, if left untended, he will worry it with the index finger of his left hand, inflaming it to the point of redness or staining it with pencil lead or pen ink. He has an irregular strawberry birthmark at the base of his spine and a gibbous moon-shaped vaccine scar affixed to his left shoulder. The sebaceous cyst, the size of a dime, just above the hairline behind Martone's left ear is not visible but can be felt, a hard nodule, in the scruff of the neck. It has been infected twice and both times lanced and drained, the wound requiring daily packing as it healed. Martone has no intentional or professional tattoos or piercings, though the back and palm of his right hand will often be scribbled with words and numbers, the result of the habit acquired when he wore a cast in high school. There are a few instances where the ink or pencil lead has gotten under the skin, resisting all his attempts at removal, leaving behind fragments of initials, icons, one half of a heart, and something that might well be an exclamation mark, a semicolon, or a simple smeared period.

CONTRIBUTOR'S NOTE

Michael Martone was born in Fort Wayne, Indiana. His mother taught freshman English at Central High School there, and his father worked for the telephone company as a switchman and clerked at nights for Pete Shinner's Package Liquor store on State Boulevard. Martone has written about accompanying his mother when he was a young child to her classes at Central, where he sat in a back corner coloring while his mother taught the novel *Silas Marner* or the play *Our Town* or, his favorite, *The Odyssey* to four different classes of teenage students. What he noticed most was that even though the material to be covered in each class was the same, each class session was always slightly different from every other. Someone would ask a question that hadn't occurred to anyone else in any of the other classes, or the discussion would stall on simple matters of definition or geography that did not seem to bother anyone else. The class after lunch was always more quiet and slow than the morning classes. His mother said the same things over and over, and every time she did it appeared as if she were saying the very same thing she said before for the very first time. It was like it had just come to her. St. Paul's Lutheran Church was just across the street and it rang out the Westminster chimes on the quarter hour. Martone's mother would always have to wait while the bells rang. Pigeons startled every time the bells struck and circled the spires of the church before settling on the limestone window-ledges outside the third-floor classroom. Once, a pigeon got caught between the real ceiling and the drop ceiling and they could hear it cooing and the sharp nails of its feet scratching the acoustic tiles above. Martone followed the custodian around the halls as he followed the journey of the trapped pigeon. At night Martone helped his mother grade papers, entering the letters in the grade book with its half pages and tiny green grid of squares. And later, when he learned to read, they read aloud together. To this day when he calls her on the phone Martone recites a line from Thorton Wilder that they rehearsed those nights of his childhood: "Am I pretty, Mamma? Am I really pretty?" His mother stayed up late after Martone went to bed, waiting for her husband to come home from the liquor store. He would bring her a Buddy Boy sandwich and an order of fries from the Azar's Big Boy, which she would wash down with a screwdriver or a 7 and 7. In the morning Martone found the wrappers in the trash. On the weekends his parents liked to have parties. His father got a good discount from Pete on cases of Falstaff and Old Crown, brewed right in town, and he splurged on all kinds of bottled spirits. Martone's mother said she liked to drink scotch best because it didn't give her a headache. At the parties Martone would get to see a house full of teachers and administrators, many of whom would later be his teachers and his school administrators, thoroughly inebriated, loud and silly and many times sick in his house. One time he woke up early to find Paul Spuller, the Central High School principal, passed out snoring on the couch. Martone's father liked to mix new drinks he had heard about from customers or read about in the advertisements at work. His birthday was on Christmas Eve, and every year on that day he got drunk going from one bar to another where the owners who knew him from the store stood him free celebratory drinks, experimenting on him with new concoctions and formulations. Daiquiris, punches, highballs, cocktails. It was a family tradition to worry about him on this day, but he always came home in time to mix the new drinks, the bizarre names of which he never could remember. His wife and his in-laws could not stay mad at him for long, and he received his annual birthday present of a bunch of switches or a sock full of coal. Martone also visited, as he did his mother's classroom, the liquor store, when his father was working there. Martone got to help bag the bottles, twisting the bag closed around the bottles' necks. His father let him eat long Seifert's pretzel sticks from the jar and slide down the delivery chute in the backroom used to move the cases and kegs of beer from the trucks into the store. Working nights, Martone's father worried about his wife home alone with Martone, so he bought an old used single-barreled shotgun for her to use as protection. She was never meant to fire it, he had told her, but to simply point it in the direction to scare away any intruder. Martone, who has a drink occasionally, most often something sweet and dyed red with grenadine or cranberry juice, now years later regards this anecdote as ironic, since Martone's father was killed one night in a botched robbery at the store while his wife waited up, grading theme papers on the stories of O. Henry, Saki, Shirley Jackson, and Guy de Maupassant. The unloaded gun was in the hall closet and stayed there until, years later, she hung it on the wall as a planter, the philodendron coaxed down the barrel and sprouting out at the muzzle and the broken-open breech.

CONTRIBUTOR'S NOTE

Michael Martone was born in Fort Wayne, Indiana, where both his mother and her father contracted colon cancer. Martone was advised by his physician to undergo a colonoscopy when he was forty-six years old, ten years before the age of the earliest onset of the disease in a family member. Upon awaking from the anesthetic of the procedure (the drug Versed, an amnesiac, was used), Martone saw his son Nick standing by the bed. Martone thanked him for coming to take him home (Martone assumed that his wife was there too). Martone told his son that his nurse had been named Linda Evans, that there had been a red automotive toolbox on wheels in the operating room, and that there was another patient scheduled to follow after he, Martone, was finished. His son looked at him and said that he knew all that, that this had been the tenth time he had heard Martone tell him the name of his nurse, the color of the toolbox, and the schedule of the outpatient clinic. Martone couldn't remember that he had, ten times apparently, awakened from the anesthesia, seen his son, Nick, and told him that his nurse was named Linda Evans, that there had been a red toolbox on wheels, probably from Sears, in the operating room, and that another patient was going to have the same procedure done right after they finished with him. The drug had not, of course, knocked him out, but only disconnected his memory so that he could not remember the discomfort of the recently completed procedure. He had been there, had felt what it felt like, but that part of his memory had been scrubbed clean by the chemicals. And then there he was, trying to start up that machine again. It was like yanking on the ignition cord of a recalcitrant lawn-mower. At last it took, sending the spool spinning centripetally in his mind, the gathering in of the things that would stick again. Martone told himself not to forget how it felt to forget. Remember, Martone remembers saying to himself. Remember how the past started up again, how it reattached to the ceaseless parade of present moments, moments you can't remember because you forgot how to remember them. What happened then? The doctor came and showed him a contact sheet with four pictures printed on it, photographs he had taken while performing the procedure on Martone. There were four pictures, souvenirs of his doctor's recent journey inside Martone with a camera and mechanical claw used to excavate the biopsied tissue. Martone remembered his doctor saying (days before the actual procedure, while reciting the disclaimers, the transparent fine print of the potential hazards of the impending procedure) that if you didn't watch it you could take a wrong turn and there you are eye to eye with somebody's spleen. Martone looked inside himself, had the opportunity, a modern oracle, to read the cursive hand of his own entrails turned inside out. His memory was spinning again, caught, and hummed along. Martone remembered.

CONTRIBUTOR'S NOTE

Michael Martone was born in Fort Wayne, Indiana. He attended graduate school in the late seventies in Baltimore at the Johns Hopkins University, where he was a fellow in the Writing Seminars. His mother was happy about this, finding it comfortable to simply tell her friends and recent acquaintances that her son went to Johns Hopkins and let them conclude, naturally, that he was going to become a doctor, a specialist of some kind no doubt, and not a writer. Martone, on his part, did take to hanging out in the biology labs at the Homewood campus, often going there directly after another intense and confusing fiction workshop. These were exciting times in biology. The labs were just developing the technologies for gene splicing and recombinant DNA experiments. This was before the imposition of federal regulations of facilities, designed to prevent the contamination of the environment by these new, genetically altered organisms. There were no P3 protocols yet, so any interested party could wander in to watch the various grad students wrangle the mutating *E. coli* under the microscopes. Martone often hung out with Eric Nelson, a grad student in biology who had taken Martone to see, for the first time in Martone's life, the ocean. They had gone to Chincoteague Island, arriving from Baltimore late at night, and had camped out in the grassy dunes. Martone had thought then that the ocean, just over the hummock of sand, sounded like motorized traffic whizzing by on a busy highway. In the morning they awoke to discover that they were being watched by a crowd of people standing some distance away. Many in the audience were taking photographs. Martone sat up in his sleeping bag. He could hear the clicks and whirrs of the automatic cameras. Soon Martone realized that he and his friend were not the subjects of the pictures but that the herd of horses snorting and cropping the grass all around them were. The famous ponies of the island! Once back at the lab, Eric showed him his newest project. He was shooting a frog gene into a strain of *E. coli* DNA. Eric explained how he used an enzyme like a blade to slice out the material. He let Martone look through the microscope. He showed Martone the stained petri dishes, the pipettes, and the test tubes. To Martone, it was all a mystery. For a while, Eric said, there had been a creature called *E. coli nelsonesis*, but then it died. Eric stayed in the lab. He often worked through the night, camping out near the emergency eyewash station. Martone went home to his apartment to attempt to write the next story to be distributed to the workshop. Back then, they used mimeography, and it took a long time to cut the stencils. If he made a mistake in typing or if he revised, he had to use a razor blade to erase the raised wax adhering to the reverse side of the typed sheet. It took a long time to correct the mistake, and he could never, no matter how hard he tried, get it all.

CONTRIBUTOR'S NOTE

Michael Martone was born in Fort Wayne, Indiana, where, after he graduated with a degree in English from Indiana University, he returned to write, in a downtown park, poetry for hire, a stunt of spontaneous composition for which he charged his audience a quarter a poem. With the money he collected Martone applied to graduate schools of creative writing, eventually being able to afford to send a baker's-dozen applications to such programs for consideration. He chose universities and colleges on both coasts, the south, the northeast, and the far west, any place but his native Midwest, since he had yet to be out of his home region for any time longer than a few days during family vacations or school field trips. While he waited to hear from the schools Martone took a road trip with Mike Wilkerson, a friend from IU also considering a graduate degree, using Mike's AMC Gremlin to tour campuses in the east. They slept in the car and made it all the way to New Haven, where they were told they would need to have three foreign languages, one of them ancient, to go to Yale. They drove around Manhattan and back and forth across the East River bridges looking for a place to park. Columbia would be too expensive and they never found NYU but did have a chance to go to a comedy club and hear a series of jokes delivered by several comics about the island of Guam, a response to an audience member reporting that Guam was the place of her birth when each comic asked the audience, "A good-looking crowd; where you from?" Martone would shout out that he was from Fort Wayne, but the comic would hear only the woman and her answer that she was born in Guam. On the way back to Indiana, Mike and Martone stopped at Indiana, Pennsylvania, at the college there, Indiana University, Pennsylvania. They did not stop because they wanted to go to graduate school there, and in fact they weren't even sure that Indiana University, Pennsylvania, had a graduate program in English or creative writing. In truth, Mike and Martone were attracted by the name. They had, growing up in Indiana, Indiana, always been aware of this other Indiana, appearing as it did in the lists of football and basketball scores, (Pennsylvania) parenthetically affixed to Indiana University to distinguish it from the Indiana University from which Mike and Martone had recently graduated. A visit to this place, a place they (up until the moment they arrived there) could only imagine, seemed inevitable, since it was just off the turnpike as they were heading west. Upon arriving, Mike and Martone immediately found their way to the campus bookstore, where they looked at all the T-shirts and sweatshirts decorated with the school's name. Martone noticed that many of the styles of fonts, the silk screening, the materials of the apparel seemed identical to those found at the other Indiana. Only when the school's seal was included did it seem different. They each bought a T-shirt. Martone told the clerk as they paid that they were from the other Indiana, and the clerk said, "We get your mail." The same thing happened in the English department when they told the secretaries they found there that they had come from the other Indiana. They said in unison, "We get your mail." Mike responded instantly, "That's why we came, to pick up the mail." On the way back to the car they stopped at a kiosk located in the middle of the campus and looked through the announcements and the advertisements posted on a bulletin board there. They met an African student and hoped to go through with him the routine they had been developing about the other Indiana and the mail, but the African student became very serious upon hearing the news that these two Americans had come from the other Indiana. "Yes," he said, "it is a big problem in my country. Students come here thinking they are going to the other Indiana and they actually are coming to this Indiana. It is worse with California. There is a California, Pennsylvania as well. I ask you, why does this happen? Why does America use the same name for many things?" Mike and Martone and the African student who didn't offer his name thought together for a moment, pondering the dilemma he posed. After a while Mike offered up an explanation. "America is so big it's run out of names," he said. In the end Martone decided to go to the Writing Seminars at the Johns Hopkins University in Baltimore after they accepted him into that program. Mike Wilkerson ended up going there as well, although he waited another year before he moved out to Maryland from Indiana. Martone had had other offers from other graduate schools. George Starbuck at Boston University had called him and asked Martone to go there. Martone thanked him for the offer but said he would probably go to Baltimore instead. "You don't want to go to Baltimore," Professor Starbuck had said. "Baltimore is the world's largest small town." Martone hadn't known then whether that was true or not, but he thought he would like to find out.

Contributor's Note

Michael Martone was born in Fort Wayne, Indiana, and was educated in the public schools there except for first, second, and part of his third-grade year, when he was a student at Queen of Angels Catholic Church School. His father and mother had been one of the first couples to marry in the new north-side parish. Their wedding was held in what had been designed as the school's gymnasium but hastily converted to a sanctuary with the promise that sometime later a real church would be built on property that was being used as a football field out back. His father was an usher and in the Holy Name and the Knights of Columbus and his mother was a member, in name if not spirit, of Queen of Angels Rosary Society. His mother, who was also a freshman English teacher at Central High School, a public school, withdrew Martone after her son developed nightmares and night terrors that she suspected were connected to his third-grade lay teacher, Mrs. Freeze, and her use of the abacus, and enrolled him in Price

Elementary two blocks away. The move made Martone's parents doubly guilty. They had already refrained from receiving the Holy Eucharist during Holy Communion because they practiced birth control. His father used condoms. Much later, after a miscarriage, Martone's mother would be prescribed birth control pills to regulate her cycle, the use of which was endorsed by Father Dave, a liberal-minded priest who wore sideburns and said the mass in English. The result of such dispensation allowed them to resume partaking in the sacrament, the sinful prophylactic of the treatment ignorable now that it had been endorsed as a medical necessity for Martone's mother's heath and well-being. But at the time they withdrew their son from parochial school, Martone's parents still wrestled with the moral dilemma of their sexual habits and the evidence of their sin, their single child there beside them in the pew each Sunday at Queen of Angels. So even while going to the public school, Martone attended weekly CCD classes, where he prepared for his confirmation, and summer school run by the Crosier Brothers. He was also instructed not to attend the classes held in the trailer at the public school, a mobile classroom sponsored by the Protestant churches that was parked nearby and provided elementary religious instruction just off school grounds and gave the occasion to pray. Martone had liked his first two years at Queen of Angels. In first grade his teacher had been Sister Mary Urban, a nun in the Order of the Most Precious Blood. The sisters there wore habits of gray skirts and guimpes with black and white wimples. In first grade Martone was the narrator in the Christmas pageant. In second grade Sister Mary Regula adored him for fainting while he fasted for his first Holy Communion, mistaking his swoon for spiritual ecstasy. Martone awoke in her gray lap and she carried him to the altar. Henceforth, Sister Mary Regula always selected Martone to be class monitor when she left the room. Once, he reported that everyone in the class except Michael Griffth and Nancy Carroll, his best friends, had been bad, but, in the confusion of Sister's returning, Michael and Nancy heard only their names called and mistook that they had been accused. From then on they loathed Martone. The fallout from this incident might have spilled over into the third grade and Mrs. Freeze's basement classroom. Martone remembers only the crowded dark room. He used the point of his pencil to slide the colored beads of his abacus up and down the rails of each of the columns. There were so many students in the class that there weren't enough workbooks to go around. Martone placed a hard plastic sheet over the page they were working on in the workbook when he got one. He would answer the questions showing through the plastic sheet using a green wax pencil. Mrs. Freeze would slowly make her way around the room, visiting the students who had the few workbooks at the time, and check the answers. Once she corrected the mistakes, writing the appropriate responses on the messy smeared sheets, she grunted her approval and instructed that the pristine workbooks should be passed on to the next student. Martone remembers then taking out his little plastic bottle of water and his crusty scrap of shoe shine cloth to clean the greasy markings from the plastic sheet. He used his fingernails to loosen the wax. His scrawled answers smeared and spread, tinting the plastic green. It took a long time to thin the wax and to wipe it into a smudged but at least translucent state, a vortex of watery green swirls and streaks. Martone believed, even then, that the plastic sheets and the cleaning thereof were metaphors for the soul and that the wax pencil markings were a tally of sins, concepts he had learned about just the year before in Sister Mary Regula's class. He scrubbed and scrubbed the plastic sheet while he waited for the workbook to be handed back to him so that he could attempt to answer the next set of questions as Mrs. Freeze made her slow way back to him to check his imperfect work.

CONTRIBUTOR'S NOTE

Michael Martone was born in Fort Wayne, Indiana, and grew up there. He graduated from North Side High School in 1973. Turning eighteen that summer, he was assigned the category of 1H by the Allen County Draft Board when his draft card arrived by mail shortly before he left home for Indiana University. There had been one last lottery drawing that he had listened to on the radio, and his birthday received a number somewhere in the middle. He was in a holding classification, and American participation in the Vietnam War appeared to be over but at the time no one knew for sure. Growing up in Fort Wayne, Indiana, during the war, Martone had helped his grandfather, who worked a second job for Ed Harz at the Standard Oil filling station downtown, close up each night, riding with his parents when they went to pick up his grandfather and take him back home. Across the street, on the ground floor of the Poagston Arms, was the suite of offices used by the county draft board. New draftees huddled on the sidewalks those nights, waiting for the buses that would take them to the induction center in Indianapolis overnight so that they would arrive first thing in the morning. His grandfather let a few of them use the office phone to call home or call girlfriends while they waited. They warmed up in the station, bought Paydays or Zero bars, bags of Planters nuts, and deposit bottles of pop that they took with them on the bus. They were only a few years older than Martone, but he always thought of them as much older. This is what he told Mr. Kern, years later, in a hotel room of the Memorial Union at Indiana University. Then Martone was a senior about to graduate, and Mr. Kern was an editor from *Life* magazine. He told the group of students gathered in his room that he was touring the country, talking with young people, trying to get a sense of who they were, what they were up to. He asked them to write letters to him in New York City. A few days later, Martone did, and in his letter he wrote how he had been designated 1H and was still holding, waiting for something to happen. It seemed, he wrote, that it was always the case that he would miss, by a few years, the important events of the time. Things happened some other place than where he was, and those things happened to some other people. He watched on television these things happen elsewhere, the war and the riots, and listened at the dinner table to his parents and grandparents fight about all the fighting. *Life*, it turned out, published part of a paragraph of Martone's letter, the only one from Indiana, embedded in columns of letters from other students from other schools. This was their special issue on "Youth Today." A few years after that, Martone found himself in New York City and called Mr. Kern, reminding him of their meeting in Bloomington and the letter he had written. For that issue Mr. Kern must have visited dozens of schools. He invited Martone up to the offices of *Life* in the same building where *Time* and *Sports Illustrated* had their offices. By then *Life* was on its last legs, publishing only special issues like the one

70

about "Youth Today" once or twice a year. It was very quiet in Mr. Kern's suite of offices. Unlike the other magazines, *Life* now had just a few permanent staff—Mr. Kern and a couple of other writers and editors who mostly culled through the back numbers of the magazine, looking for interesting photographs they could reuse in the retrospective theme annuals. Martone considers his letter to *Life* magazine to be his first publication, and Mr. Kern said he was very happy to have played a part in his career. When Martone told him that he wanted to be a writer, Mr. Kern mistook the statement as an application for a position with the company. He quickly told Martone to look around, things there were only going to get worse. The office window looked west, and they were high enough to see the river and the Jersey shore beyond. Martone had taken a train from Fort Wayne to get to the city. Fort Wayne was somewhere out there to the west. They talked about Mr. Kern's visit to Indiana and schools that Martone might attend in the future until the setting sun lit up the room. Mr. Kern went with Martone back down to the lobby and walked out with him to the Avenue of the Americas, where he wished Martone the best of luck and where they then said their final good-byes. In the doorway, Mr. Kern turned and actually waved to Martone before he turned again and went back in the building.

CONTRIBUTOR'S NOTE

Michael Martone was born in Fort Wayne, Indiana, which is located on the confluence of three rivers—the St. Joseph, the St. Marys, and the Maumee. The city is situated on the summit of the eastern continental divide, giving it its nickname, the Summit City. The elevation, however, is only 765 feet above sea level, and the variation between the Atlantic and Mississippi basins is, in Fort Wayne, a matter of a few feet either way. Martone regards this unique topography as a contributing influence upon his aesthetic. The fact that the tributaries of the Maumee, flowing from the north and east, contribute to a river that then flows back the same way, north and east, astounds him. That and the fact that the river that issues from the confluence of the St. Joseph and St. Marys rivers was not named, for some reason, the Jesus.

Contributor's Note

Michael Martone, an orphan, was born in Story County, Iowa, and was raised there by five women—seniors at Iowa State College, majoring in home economics—in what was then known as the Home Management House. The Home Management House, a freestanding, prairie-style bungalow on the edge of campus, served as a laboratory and practicum for the graduating students who lived there their final year. Monthly, the students took turns performing and being tested on various tasks. One would do the housecleaning; one, the shopping for food and the preparing of the menus; one, the making of clothes; one, the managing of the household furnishings and finances. They were given "money" by the dean, and they then purchased furniture and food from the college store, their budgeting and interior-decorating skills rigorously assessed. One student each month was assigned the baby—bathing it, dressing it, feeding it, changing it, rocking it to sleep each night. The baby, a month after birth, was selected from the new batch of orphaned infants at the county home outside Nevada. Swaddled and placed in a wicker clothes-basket, the newborn was driven over to the school by a sheriff's deputy and a home matron and there handed over to the new class of students, who gathered expectantly on the house's newly painted front porch. The college newspaper always sent a photographer to record the arrival, five excited coeds jointly holding the bundle. Martone was one of those babies. He remembers nothing of his first year of life in the Home Management House. Shortly afterward, he was adopted by the Martones, a childless couple from Indiana, who died in a car crash when Martone was a junior majoring in ice cream at Purdue. Orphaned once again, he learned of his natal care during an aborted search for his birth mother. That summer he secured an internship with the Schwann Company, a door-to-door distributor of frozen foods and convenience items, and returned to Iowa to drive a route truck over the rural farm market roads. His clientele included many farm women who had majored in Home Economics, spending their senior year at the Home Management House. He would coax from them their stories of their time there as he sat at kitchen tables writing up orders over expertly prepared coffee and home-baked quick breads. Once, he was shown a clipping of a baby's delivery, the picture grainy and the paper yellowed with age. Was this Martone? From the various reports he pieced together, Martone became reasonably satisfied with the identity of four of the five students who nurtured him that first year, and he spent the rest of the summer and most of the fall—he took a leave from Purdue—searching for what he began to believe were his mothers. Two turned up dead. He visited the grave of the first near Lake Okoboji. From a pay phone at the Jones Cafe in Eldon he talked with the still distraught husband of the second, who refused to see him. As they talked it became more difficult to hear the husband's perfunctory replies, and Martone realized that the farm was still on a party line. As the widower's neighbors, one by one, began to listen, the voltage on the line would drop. This helped to explain the taciturn response. The man, trained by years of such eavesdropping, now coupled his answers to his obvious grief. Martone never could find the other mother. The trail petered out at an abandoned farm near the Quad Cities. He did have a chance to speak with Mary Jane Brown, who farmed near Turin in western Iowa in the Loess Hills, who remembered him as an easy baby, saying she should know, since she had four more of her own. She couldn't recall the fifth girl's name, so she was no help there. She said her real strength had been in the kitchen. She hated to clean and could not forget boiling the diapers and watching them freeze on the line out back of the house that winter. She was happy that one of her months with the baby had been in the spring. She was already engaged to Thayer and they would marry that June. "I'd sit on the porch," she said, "and rock you in the chair I made Anne buy." She would hold his little hand up and wave it at the students passing on the way to class. Martone stayed for dinner and met the rest of the Brown family, including Jane, the oldest daughter, who was then a senior at Iowa State University, where she was a senior majoring in home economics and whom he later married, against the wishes of her parents, in a small civil ceremony at the courthouse in Nevada.

ACKNOWLEDGMENT

The author wishes to acknowledge the invaluable contribution of his first editor, who called him one day and offered to publish his first book. The call came as a complete surprise. The editor, who was also a writer, had visited the university in Ames, Iowa, where the author was then teaching, to give a reading of the editor's own work. The editor had said to all the writers in town who came to hear the editor read to send him "your best work." A dozen people must have followed the editor's suggestion and sent work to him at his office in New York, including the author, who sent two stories that would be the last he heard of that. But the editor had called offering to do a book of stories based on reading the two stories the author had sent. Of course, the editor said, you will have to write many more stories in order to make a collection. The editor had come to Ames, Iowa, after wrangling an invitation from a colleague of the author who had had, years before, a book accepted by the editor but which was never published because the

79

editor left that publishing house to become a magazine editor. In spite of that, the editor stayed in touch with the author's colleague, cajoling the author's college to invite him, the editor, out to Ames, Iowa, to give a reading of his, the editor's, fiction. It was the history of the author's colleague's business dealings with the editor that made the author wary when the editor called him later to say he wanted to publish a book of the author's stories. That and the way the editor persisted, calling upon his colleague to invite the editor to give a reading. The editor always insisted in the request, in a manner that one could not tell whether the editor was kidding or not, that the compensation for the reading should include, though not be limited to, an introduction of the editor to an interested and attractive coed of the college or perhaps two coeds, twins being the most preferable arrangement. Knowledge of this and other things, such as the fact that the editor had been the subject of a thinly disguised roman à clef in which the character who was supposed to be the editor routinely offended and/or damaged a whole list of writers through unkept promises, broken contracts, and mean-spirited tit for tat, had primed the author's suspicions about the opportunity the editor had proffered on the phone. In fact, the author was surprised that the editor had survived having elevated the hopes of so many other authors with the promise of publication only to dash such hopes over and over. The author knows that the mere mention of the editor's name will elicit from writers new variations on the themes of the asymmetry of power and the betrayal of excited desires. To this day the author does not know how the book did in fact make it into print, given the anecdotal evidence of the editor's other dealings with other authors and other books. The author visited New York and sat in the office of the editor while the editor edited the author's book. When he was finished he told the author to transcribe all of the editor's edits onto a clean unedited copy of the author's book so that there would be no mistake, the editor's hand being sometimes illegible, when the work was forwarded to production. The author was to have a hand in the final crafting of the book and in so doing better appreciate the genius of the editor by tracing the pattern of his emendations. But first the author was to walk with the editor down Fifth Avenue to Brooks Brothers to return a sweater the editor had purchased for his son. As they walked the crowded sidewalk the editor was careful to point out to the author, as they would approach the oncoming flow of traffic, the women with whom the editor had had amorous affairs. What the editor said was, "I did her," pointing at a woman walking by. The author acknowledges that the editor "did" many "her"s present at that moment on the Fifth Avenue sidewalk in New York City. Years later, after the editor lost interest in the author and the author moved on to other books with other editors, the author had the occasion to visit Washington College on Maryland's Eastern Shore. There, the home of the large endowed program for writers, the author toured the house set aside for student offices and classrooms and the antique printing presses used to create attractive posters announcing the visiting writers and their performance schedule at the college. Over the years the posters had been framed and hung on the walls of the house. The author noticed that some of the posters were hung upside down and asked his guide about that. The author was told that the visitors announced on those posters were the visitors the students did not like. On the second floor the author noticed that one poster hung not only upside down but also back to front, thereby making it impossible to see whom the poster represented. The author asked whom that poster represented and was told that this was a visitor who was really disliked. The author was asked to guess who that might be, and without thinking the author said the name of the editor of his first book. The author would like to acknowledge that it was indeed the editor he has acknowledged here who holds that place of honor.

Contributor's Note

Michael Martone was born in Fort Wayne, Indiana. His father worked for the telephone company and his mother was an English teacher at Central High School. In order to augment her teaching salary, every Christmas, for as long as Martone can remember, his mother performed dramatic readings of Charles Tazewell's children's book *The Littlest Angel* for women's clubs, PTAs, church groups, office parties, luncheons, neighborhood open houses, seasonal brunches, class reunions, retreats, even baby and bridal showers. Indeed, the Christmas season was always initiated for Martone when he would catch his mother a few days before Thanksgiving, rehearsing the text in a corner of the living room. "Once upon a time," it began, "oh, many, many years ago as time is calculated by men—but which was only yesterday in the Celestial Calendar of heaven...." Martone does not remember exactly when it was that he memorized most of the story, listening to his mother practice and perform it through his childhood.

But even today, years later, fragments of the text will occur to him while he is trying to recall something else. As a supplement to her income, his mother's presentations were not very lucrative. She called it "the handkerchief circuit," compensation of embroidered hankies being presented in appreciation by her hosts along with an invitation to help herself to the cucumber sandwiches, cookies, and cheese ball with crackers. The handkerchiefs were lovely but completely impractical as handkerchiefs. His mother kept them in a top drawer of her dresser and sometimes spread them out on her bed to show them to her son. Martone remembers one particularly, sinews of glossy red thread forming a cardinal perched amid the green stitched leaves of the tulip poplar, Indiana's state bird and tree. His mother had first memorized the book while in college. The story concerned the littlest angel in heaven, who was having a difficult time being an angel of any dimension in heaven. A reoccurring image was of the Littlest Angel chasing his halo, a golden hoop, through the streets of paradise. The story explains the appearance of the star over Bethlehem on the first Christmas. The Littlest Angel's humble gift to the Christ child is chosen above all the others offered by the choirs of seraphim and cherubim, saints and martyrs, and transformed into the star. Giving *The Littlest Angel* all those years, Martone's mother had evolved a whole repertoire of gestures to accompany the words. When the story reported the angel's age in detail, his mother would count off the time using various combinations of her fingers for the years, months, weeks, days, hours, minutes, and seconds. Martone always liked this part of the story no matter how many times he saw her do it. It made him conscious of his own age and the passing of time. The Littlest Angel's gift, the one that was transformed because of its purity into the star over Bethlehem, was a box of treasures he had collected while a mortal little boy. He had hidden the box of butterfly wings, marbles, crayons, and carved wooden dolls before he died, and an understanding angel in heaven facilitated the Littlest Angel's retrieval of the treasure. Martone believes that he might be, in his memory, confusing this box from the story with the box shown in the opening credits of *To Kill a Mockingbird*. *The Littlest Angel* is not one of the better-known Christmas stories due to its religious emphasis, perhaps. Martone, when he was a child not much older than the Littlest Angel, often attended his mother's performances, sitting in the front row and following along with the recitation. And later he suffered the adoration of the women audience members as they congratulated and thanked his mother. When he didn't go with his mother to her readings, he would stay home and watch the more secular and successful Christmas shows on television. Martone had been a child during the golden age of such specials. There was *The Grinch Who Stole Christmas,* animated by Chuck Jones, *A Charlie Brown Christmas,* with the jazzy score by Vince Guaraldi, the stop-action animation of *Rudolph the Red-Nosed Reindeer* with the voice of Burl Ives, who also did *Frosty the Snowman,* and his favorite, the *Mr. Magoo Christmas Carol,* with Mr. Magoo as Scrooge. By that time, too, he had his own box of treasures, a cigar box his father had given him, filled with his own toys and trinkets, worthless objects that had taken on meanings and memories. Martone liked to arrange the items kept there while he watched the television shows and waited for his mother's return. Years later Martone teased his mother, who continued to "give" (as she liked to say) *The Littlest Angel* up until the day she died, about the lack of compensation. The unused dainty handkerchiefs continued to pile up in the top drawer of her dresser. Martone inherited the dowry and keeps them now in his own dresser. His mother, in retaliation for his teasing, always asked Martone why he always brought this up. And, she asked, just how much, by the way, had he made from his own little stories published over the years in little magazines or what grand remuneration had he garnered performing these anecdotes for small though appreciative gatherings in classrooms and college lecture halls.

CONTRIBUTOR'S NOTE

Michael Martone was born in Fort Wayne, Indiana, and never left the state for more than one week at a time until attending graduate school at the Johns Hopkins University in Baltimore. There one day, while walking up Charles Street, he stopped to watch the filming of a scene from the movie *Diner*. Then, Martone did not know it, since all he saw were the accoutrements of film production—the big theatrical lights, many nonchalant electrical cables, chocked elaborate trailers, generators on flatbeds, actual safari chairs, a camera on a dolly. Or at least he imagined that it was a dolly. Martone didn't know what he was watching. It might have been a commercial being filmed. So Martone was pleasantly surprised when a year or so later while watching the movie *Diner* he recognized the scene where Mickey Rourke's character is intimidated in the doorway of the beauty salon as the one he had witnessed being filmed that day. He had been across the street, in front of Louie's Bookstore and Cafe, watching the scene being filmed, though he couldn't see the real action, since it took place beneath some stairs and in a doorway below street level, but he had seen the action around the action. The call for silence, the huddle around the camera pointed down toward the stairwell, and an old model car slowly rolling by in what was, in the film, the background. A few years earlier, when Martone was still in Indiana and a student at Indiana University, he had been an extra in the movie being filmed in Bloomington that summer, called *Breaking Away*. Martone wasn't really an extra but more of an extra extra, one person in the large crowd gathered for the stadium shooting of the climactic final bicycle race. The race takes up a lot of time during the film, but actual filming of the scene took even longer. When Martone watches the movie (it is a minor cult classic that shows up surprisingly often on television) he tries to see himself in the blurred crowd behind the racing bicycles. He wore a red and white striped shirt and jeans. A few years later, after he returned from Baltimore to Indiana, Martone was also a member of the crowd used in the movie *Hoosiers*. He was in the stands with the same crowd but in the movie they were made to look like different crowds in different gyms as the basketball team, through a montage of games, proceeded through the winning season. He also was in the stands at Hinkle Fieldhouse, where they filmed the climactic final game and where an assistant director directed them on how to act like an excited crowd. Martone also looks for himself when he watches *Hoosiers* on television. It gets shown often during basketball season, especially in March during the tournament time. Martone wore a blue oxford cloth button-down shirt and jeans and sat up near the large windows that cast most everyone there in silhouette. And a few years later still, Martone answered a casting call for extras to fill a stadium for the movie *Rudy*, about a football player at Notre Dame. During the shooting Martone sat near the place in the stadium where he, as a child growing up in

Indiana, had sat when his father took him to real football games at Notre Dame. In those real crowds he watched real games, had seen Roger Staubach play for Navy and O. J. Simpson play for Southern Cal. For the movie they moved the crowd around the big bowl of the stadium to make it appear on screen as if the stadium were entirely full. When he watches the movie now, Martone searches for himself in the background. He wore a brown stadium coat and jeans. *Rudy* is shown routinely in Indiana. The local television stations must own their own copies. It is shown especially during the football season. Martone watches it and the other movies in their seasons with his father and mother in the TV room of the house where he grew up. His mother is convinced that she has found him in *Breaking Away*. His father is too distracted by the inaccuracies of the recorded football and basketball plays to notice, recalling the times he was in the stands watching famous, historic games. Michael Martone grew up in Fort Wayne, Indiana. Martone has grown up in Indiana watching these movies about growing up in Indiana. He likes thinking about being, while growing up in Indiana, caught at certain ages and places in time there. "There you are," his mother says as the local boy in the movie races past in the foreground on his bicycle. Martone, now in his late forties, watches many movies shown on late night television and on the cable channels dedicated to showing only movies. He routinely scans the Fort Wayne newspapers for news of yet another nearby location being filmed, another take on life here in Indiana, another possible request for extras. He feels, now, that he has an aptitude for the part and, certainly, the experience to wait and hope.

Contributor's Note

Michael Martone was born in Fort Wayne, Indiana, and grew up there. He has taught literature and writing at several universities, including the University of Alabama, Syracuse University, Harvard University, and Iowa State University. While at Iowa State he attended the annual conference on Midwestern literature, driving to East Lansing with Doug Pate, a reference librarian who was working on an annotated bibliography of Iowa authors. An amusing aspect of the annual Midwestern literature conference was that every paper delivered included a lengthy introduction by its author arguing the exact location of the Midwest and thereby justifying the inclusion of this subject in the disputed region and, hence, the merit of the paper to follow. It seemed that the question of where the Midwest actually was was never really settled by its experts, and the conferees hurried past the formalities of their definitions to get to the heart of their papers, i.e., their authors and the books they really wanted to talk about. On that occasion

Martone thought that the Midwest was made up mostly of the states that have universities in the Big Ten athletic conference and maybe Nebraska, and he said so when he gave his paper on the writings of Herbert Hoover. On the way to the conference Pate and Martone stopped at the Hoover birthplace in West Branch to stretch their legs and buy some postcards at the cafe where they had breakfast. It was a long car trip to Michigan made longer but more interesting by taking US 30, the old Lincoln Highway, all the way to Chicago. Here and there along the way, Martone saw the decaying road markers with the silhouette of the president or the big "L" stenciled on red, white, and blue painted boards. Often the road paralleled the mainline of the Chicago and Northwestern railroad, and they would pace along with long trains of covered hopper cars the colors of after-dinner mints. They commented to each other often on how that spring's plowing and planting was progressing, the many red and green tractors pulling clouds of dust behind them. Martone learned that his companion had just returned from a weekend with the National Guard, a reconnaissance and military intelligence regiment that met at an armory in Des Moines. Martone was surprised to hear that the unit was made up mostly of librarians like Don Pate, and instead of camping out or firing their weapons, the guardsmen sat around in the gym and pored over newspapers and magazines from Soviet bloc nations. Pate told Martone that he really shouldn't be telling him this, but one weekend a month they got together to update their files on the military officers in the opposing communist camp. Pate was charged with keeping tabs on a captain of a reserve intelligence unit in the Ukraine. The captain had a wife and two children and liked to fly radio-controlled airplanes. They knew this, Pate told him, because of a letter the captain had written to a hobbyist magazine published in Kiev. Each month Pate, who was a captain, tracked the movements of his target. One month he would be in Siberia. Another month Pate would find him on the Black Sea or on maneuvers in the steppe. Pate said he had built quite a dossier on his subject and had access every once in a while to the new computer databases compiled by the Department of Defense. Everyone in Pate's unit had a comparable assignment. They spent the final hours of their weekend together in Des Moines typing their updated reports in the cavernous gym, the clatter of their key strikes echoing around the room. Pate and Martone stopped again, this time in Dixon, Illinois, the boyhood home of then President Reagan, to have lunch at a busy cafe nearby. They ordered breaded pork tenderloins, the deep-fried meat patty as large as the platter on which it was served. It was there that Pate told Martone that he, Pate, was being watched as well by a counterpart in the Soviet Union, the very captain in the Ukraine that he, Pate, followed. Martone thought how strange it was that this lunch in Dixon, that the paper to be given at the Midwestern Literature Conference, that the whole trip on the old Lincoln Highway would soon be duly recorded and analyzed half a world away. Martone would enter the archive, his name noted and perhaps a few facts, such as his birth in Fort Wayne, Indiana, and his expertise in the writings of Herbert Hoover. Martone shared a room with Pate at the conference. Martone was in bed early after the long trip while Pate, saying that he was still too wired from the drive, wrote postcards at the desk, hoping the light wouldn't bother Martone and keep him awake.

CONTRIBUTOR'S NOTE

Michael Martone was born in Fort Wayne, Indiana, and grew up there. As a child he was, his mother always said, a handful. Once, in a fit of anger, Martone smashed Tony Kent's cap-firing plastic tommy-gun on the metal leg of the swing set, breaking the toy in two. Tony, a stutterer, had a speech therapist instruct him to repeat under his breath everything he said. He stood there crying, "I can't believe you did that!" then whispering, "I can't believe you did that." A few weeks later, Martone bit his mother's friend Lorraine Davis's son on the arm. But when Martone, who was five, pounded Mark Schomberg, who was the same age, on the head with a whiffle ball bat, his parents had reached the end. Exasperated, they did something drastic. Without thinking, they hustled Martone off to the two-toned Chevy Impala and drove him to the Catholic orphanage, St. Vincent de Paul's, on Wells Street. The car was strangely quiet. Martone's anger spent, he sat still in the back seat during the drive down Spring Street past

Red Rarrick's Appliances with all the televisions on in the window. His parents, in the front seat, murmured below the engine's noise, staring straight ahead. They approached the main building of the orphanage by means of a long tree-lined driveway from Wells Street. The buff brick buildings were built in a Moorish style with screened balconies supported by delicate twisting columns, gracefully arched windows, and red tiled roofs. Martone remembers being pulled from the car by his mother and given a little shove toward the carved wooden gate entrance before him. Behind him, the car door closed, and Martone heard the motor of the Chevy rev a bit and the tires crush the pea stones in the drive. He turned and ran after the car already easing down the lane. The taillights blinked on and a door opened. Martone climbed back into the back seat and huddled on the floor well, his head pillowed on the driveshaft bump. During the ride back home he remembers looking up through the rear window at the passing canopy of trees, the crisscrossing wires overhead and the floating clouds. He thought then, and believes now, that he saw the face of a stern nun in the cutout of the orphanage's gate like the head in the window of a television in the window of Red Rarrick's store. This story embarrassed Martone's parents, and Martone enjoyed repeating it in his parents' presence to people who had never heard it. His mother always said to remember how young they were then, how they didn't know what else to do. Joseph Geha, a friend of Martone, remarked once that Martone had told him the story about the orphanage six or seven times. It surprised Martone when he said this. Martone thought that he had just thought of that time when he was five and his parents, at the end of their rope, took him to St. Vincent's Villa and left him with the nuns. It surprised Martone even more that Joe's observation suggested an obsessive quality to the memory, a memory that Martone believes he regarded as simply a lighthearted, funny anecdote from his youth. Joe, who is a storywriter and had been in group therapy, said often that we all have these stories we come back to. We worry them. We tell them over and over without knowing we are doing it, trying to make sense out of our lives. Martone returned to the orphanage a few years after his parents threatened to leave him there. His father helped coach the Central Catholic football team that used the field in the back of the property for practice. On a hill nearby there was a three-story concrete statue of Mary. Martone sat at Mary's feet on the head of the serpent that her feet were crushing to wait for his father and watch the scrimmage below. Occasionally, the orphans, who had a playground nearby, came over to check him out. Then they would climb up the folds of Mary's gown and perch on her head until a nun, very much like the one Martone remembers in the doorway, came over to tell them to get down. Later still, when Martone was a member of his high school Key Club, a service organization, he came back to the orphanage as part of a philanthropic event. The Key Club took a group of orphans to a Fort Wayne Komets hockey game. Each club member was assigned an orphan. Martone sat in the stands of the Memorial Coliseum, watching the game with his orphan, who turned to Martone and said that he would sure like a puck to take back to the home. "Go tell them we're orphans," the orphan said, "they'll give you anything." A few years after that the orphanage closed, and the Catholic Church sold the buildings to the YWCA and other nonprofit agencies like the local public radio station that built studios in one of the old dormitories. Martone has returned several times to the grounds of the old orphanage to do interviews on the radio or make appearances on shows that discuss books the local library suggests everyone should read. The grounds of the Villa look pretty much the same as when it was an orphanage. The Y has put up a lighted sign in the sweeping front lawn. The football field, the playground, and Mary are gone, replaced by the radio station's antenna on the hill.

Every time Martone returns to talk of the books he has written or the ones he has read, he tells the story about the time his parents, desperate, dropped him off there at the orphanage. He does this (tells the story) for the benefit of the studio engineer as he checks the levels of the microphones before the broadcast begins. And on her deathbed, right before she died of natural causes, Martone's mother remembered the day, when, in a fit of rage and foolishness, she took her son to the orphanage, and she asked him then whether he remembered that day too.

CONTRIBUTOR'S NOTE

Michael Martone was born in Fort Wayne, Indiana, and grew up there. When Martone was in high school it was often commented upon by family, friends, acquaintances, and even total strangers that he looked like Paul McCartney, one of the Beatles, a British rock and roll band that had recently visited America for the first time, selling records, playing concerts, and appearing on television programs such as *The Ed Sullivan Show*. Soon after that, the Beatles' first movie, *A Hard Day's Night*, was released. By that time Martone had let his dark brown hair grow longer, like most of the other boys in his school, and the longer hair increased the occasions when he received comments about his uncanny resemblance to the singer/songwriter. He imagined that he could see something around his eyes, the drape of his lids, he supposed, or there was an echo of the angle of McCartney's chin in Martone's own. But it was mostly the hair, he supposed, falling straight down his broad forehead to his overly bushy brow, which he had only recently begun shaving on the bridge of his nose. Coincidentally, Martone was involved with a short-lived cover band inspired by the success of the Beatles' performance in the movie. The new band would lip synch the songs and imitate the Beatles' goofy antics, being pursued through the neighborhood by their screaming younger sisters. His bandmates, excited by Martone's evolving mimicry of one of their role models, urged Martone to take up the electric bass and begin memorizing the lyrics from *Meet the Beatles*. Oddly, and for reasons too complicated to explain here, Martone preferred to play the part of the band's manager, Brian Epstein, whose looks nobody then had any idea of, and stay backstage safely out of sight. Over time, Martone's and McCartney's shared facial characteristics began to diverge. For one thing, Martone gained weight, his cheeks becoming even fuller and rounder than they had been, his neck merging with his chin and jawline. McCartney's face, on the other hand, began to sag, and the folds under his eyes grew deeper in shadow, the lids more hooded, setting the eyes themselves deeper in their sockets. There came a point when the casual mentions concerning the similarity of their shared appearance ceased altogether. People would stare in startled confusion into Martone's face when he mentioned that once other people thought he looked like Paul McCartney. "I don't see it," they would say. There was a time, then, as he approached adulthood, when Martone, as far as he could ascertain, looked like no one but his parents. His mother always said that if you broke Martone's face in two, the top half favored his father, especially the nose and eyes, but that the lips and chin were undoubtedly her contribution. Soon Martone began to receive more and more comments that would draw a comparison between his appearance and that of an emerging character actor from Chicago named Joe Mantegna, whose face, of course, was memorable but whose name unfortunately was not. Mr. Mantegna was, often for Martone's informants, the guy, you know, the actor in *Things Change* or *House of Games* or, later, the last *Godfather.* "Joe Mantegna?" Martone would answer once the pattern had become clear. And the resemblance was and is remarkable. Once, Martone himself had to look twice at a film-still printed in his local newspaper. What, he thought at the time, am I doing in the newspaper? The similarity is most striking from a certain angle and stronger in profile. For some roles Mr. Mantegna will grow a beard, and Martone, whose hair now is best described as salt and pepper, believes that the actor probably colors his. Recently, another name, an actor again, is mentioned when people are moved to compare Martone's looks to others. Adam Arkin, the son of the actor Alan Arkin, who, he, Adam, resembles, comes up almost as frequently as Joe Mantegna as someone Martone looks like. Or when someone is searching for Joe Mantegna's name to tell Martone that he looks like him, he or she will say, you know, it is the actor who looks like the actor who is Alan Arkin's son. Martone suspects that it is the eyes, the shape of the head, the hair where his face and the faces of these actors intersect. At a wedding reception recently, the mother of the bride commented in the receiving line that Martone had George Clooney's eyes, and, later that night, Martone pondered this new information. It just so happened that *One Fine Day* starring George Clooney was being shown on television. Martone stared at George Clooney's eyes as they appeared on the television screen before him, attempting to see the likeness, but found, perhaps because he was a bit drunk from the wedding reception, that it was very difficult to look at someone's eyes or a picture of someone else's eyes, then look at your own eyes in a mirror in order to determine whether the two sets of eyes look in any way the same. The eyes on the screen and in the mirror kept moving. Secretly, Martone believes that he looks most like a cartoon character named Fred Flintstone. The particulars all seem to be a match. The thick neck, the shadow of the beard, the dark eyes and hair. Martone realizes that his self-image is probably a distortion, a projection of his own insecurities about his real appearance, but he can't help himself. And he isn't too surprised when, in an unguarded moment, he asks someone he has just met whether he or she doesn't think that he, Martone, isn't the spitting image of Fred Flintstone, and the acquaintance squints and says, "Yes, I can see that."

A Contributor's Note

Provided by the Author, Who Gives Permission for Its Use in Case His Contest Entry of 500 Words or Less Is Selected for Reprinting in a Magazine or in the Event of the Necessity of Creating, by the Contest's Sponsors, a Press Release Announcing the Results of the Judging

Michael Martone was born in Fort Wayne, Indiana, where from an early age he entered contests and sweepstakes he found advertised on the side panels of cereal boxes or listed in his local newspaper. Often he was required to collect and send box-tops from specially marked packages or proof-of-purchase seals along with filled-in application forms. He would fill out pads of entry forms by hand to comply with the instruction in the fine print against photocopying or employing any means of mechanical reproduction. He wrote his name, address, and phone number over and over so that anytime he picked up a pen or pencil he automatically began to print (the instructions always asked that he

103

print) his contact information. His mother tracked his winnings. She kept a scrapbook she labeled *My Achievements* where she taped in copies of coupons and receipts sent to Martone to redeem prizes and awards, the congratulatory letters, and the original game rules. After all those blank entry blanks, Martone gravitated to the contests asking for a bit of his creative effort, a drawing or a brief essay as well as the completion of the requisite entry form. The essays were his favorite, since he couldn't draw to save his life. The rules always asked for the submission to be of a certain word length, 100 words or less or 250 words or less. That formulation of words in the guidelines always disturbed Martone's mother, who was an English teacher. She corrected the instructions, in red pencil no less, inserting "fewer" above the crossed-out "less." Martone liked the puzzle of the number of words, liked using every word allowed, liked to imagine that someone somewhere actually read his little essays, counted the words as he or she did so, even though Martone suspected, quite early, that his efforts were simply more elaborate entry forms. The winners, runners-ups, and honorable mentions were all, no doubt, selected by the usual method of random drawing. Martone became adept at the form. His specialty was the use of words compounded by employing a hyphen, such as "proof-of-purchase" or "runners-up." The grafting counted as one word instead of two or three. In high school he obsessively entered such essay contests sponsored by civic organizations and church groups, soliciting his thoughts on patriotic themes, good citizenship, personal health, and public sanitation. He often won contests and was invited to luncheon meetings of enthusiastic Rotarians, Lions, Zontas, and Veterans who appreciated the brevity of the winning essays. Years later, Martone is still entering contests, writing tiny paragraphs of prose. Now, oddly, these contests require that he pay to enter, more like a state lottery but with better odds. Martone likes using long titles. He figures those words don't count.

Today, he writes on his computer. It has a word count feature. He pushes one button, and he automatically knows where he stands. His mother no longer has to count the words by hand, looking up at him at the end and whispering, "Fewer."

CONTRIBUTOR'S NOTE

Michael Martone was born in Fort Wayne, Indiana, and grew up there attending the public schools. The first two and a half years of his college education were spent at Butler University in Indianapolis. When he attempted to transfer to Indiana University in Bloomington, he discovered he would lose twenty hours of advanced-placement credits that Butler accepted, mostly freshman and sophomore introduction courses in the biological, physical, and social sciences, along with math and history. Instead of making up the courses in the huge lecture halls of the main campus surrounded by hundreds of freshman, Martone decided to begin by taking the smaller classes on the regional campus in Fort Wayne, where he could save money at the same time by living with his grandparents in their brick house overlooking Hamilton Park, not far from the campus. This arrangement made Martone happy, too, since he secretly believed that his grandparents wouldn't be alive much longer and that they and he would mutually benefit from the close, loving proximity of the generations. In reality Martone's grandparents lived a good fifteen years more after he moved out the following fall to finish his degree in Bloomington in the spring of 1977. While living with his grandparents and going to school Martone worked at Reader's World Bookstore in Glenbrook Mall, tried out for the campus production of *The Threepenny Opera,* and was cast as one of the thugs in the chorus. Martone, as part of his character for the play, had to give up shaving, and his shaggy appearance put a strain on the living arrangement early in the semester. When not working or rehearsing or studying Martone attended speeches and special programs on the campus. One such evening was a debate between his professor of cultural anthropology and a minister on the subjects of evolution, the nature of science, and creation. In the middle of the debate someone in a gorilla suit arrived at the hall and ambled up to a seat on the aisle in one of the front rows, where it sat thoughtfully listening to the speeches. He also heard Flo Kennedy say that she needed a man like a fish needed a bicycle. Martone's favorite guest was George Plimpton, the participatory journalist who had written books about playing professional baseball and football, tennis and hockey, and even playing timpani in a philharmonic orchestra. Martone had begun to think of himself as a writer of poetry and fiction. This had been one of the reasons for transferring to Indiana University in the first place. Because he now thought of himself as a writer, Martone also knew that Mr. Plimpton edited a magazine called the *Paris Review.* Martone had sent some poems (they had been about death) to the magazine for consideration, and he had the rejection slip, which he used as a bookmark, in his introductory sociology textbook. The questioners in the audience that evening all asked Mr. Plimpton how it had felt to play goalie on a hockey team or what it was like to punt in a football game. What was it like to act in a movie? He answered all these questions with amusing anecdotes of his experience. No one else seemed to be aware of Mr. Plimpton's literary connection. Near the end of the session, Martone asked whether Mr. Plimpton would, as publisher and editor, ever consider allowing an amateur such as Martone himself to edit an issue of the *Paris Review*. No, Mr. Plimpton said, he hadn't considered it, and it was an idea that didn't appeal to him. Next question, he said. Years later, Martone, who has been published in *Antaeus*, *North American Review*, *Shenandoah*, *Ascent*, *Crazyhorse*, and many other magazines, sent this contributor's note to the *Paris Review*, still edited by Mr. Plimpton.

Contributor's Note

Michael Martone was born in Fort Wayne, Indiana, and almost died there five years later while having his tonsils removed at Parkview Hospital. Martone had been a sickly child, and his pediatrician, named Dr. Savage, suggested that much of the illness had been caused by his underactive tonsils, the absorption of toxic substances within the mysterious lymphoid tissue masses lodged in the back of Martone's throat. His mother, weary of the recurrence of strep throat infections and bouts of rheumatic fever in her son, willingly agreed with the doctor's diagnosis and therapy. She prepared her son for his visit to the hospital by working into his bedtime reading a book called *My Visit to the Hospital* that in words and illustrations narrated for a child Martone's age what to expect from an inpatient visit of minor surgery such as a tonsillectomy or removal of the adenoids. Martone was also going to have his adenoids removed. "Might as well," Dr. Savage had said. Martone's mother, after reading the book to him several nights running, helped him pack and unpack his new canvas satchel gym bag with the essentials he would need for what the doctor and the book had promised would be an overnight stay. Martone folded and unfolded his pajamas and a pair of clean underwear, a T-shirt, a pair of jeans, slippers, and balled-up socks. He had a new toothbrush and a miniature tube of toothpaste and a tiny bar of soap. His mother painted her fingernails bright red, and she let Martone sniff the ether drifting from the shell-shaped bottle of fingernail polish remover that she used. Martone thought it smelled sweet and seemed effervescent but wasn't. Martone, while he inhaled, stared at the box of fingernail polish bottles, all in shades of red that had looked, when he had looked before, all the same but now appeared to be all just slightly different in hue and brightness and tone. His mother read their red names—pomegranate, apple, fire engine, tulip, sunset, tomato, beet, and blood. All the bottles had different tops capped with spires of clear plastic shafts shaped like golf tees, propeller blades, letter openers, and flower petals. She painted Martone's own fingernails after she cut them in anticipation of going to the hospital, painted each fingernail a different shade of red, and the next night, while he looked at his book again, she removed the lacquers, letting him inhale the residue of ether on his fingers when he went to sleep that night. Martone had been told of the diet he would endure in the hospital, a diet made up of Popsicle, as his throat heeled. His mother prompted him to list all the flavors he could and he did, settling on cherry, raspberry, and strawberry—the red ones. The night before Martone was scheduled to enter the hospital to get his tonsils and adenoids removed, his mother took him to see the priest at Queen of Angels, Father Faber. Father, in his vestment, had Martone kneel at the communion rail and blessed Martone's throat by placing two unlit candles crossed beneath his chin. The church was empty and dark. Only the lights above the tabernacle and the exit doors were left on.

Father Faber muttered in Latin and rubbed Martone's lips with oil, patting him on his head when he said he was through, asking him what kind of ice cream he would ask for. Later that night Martone's mother told him the story of St. Blaise. She also told him of the time Martone's father had gotten a fish bone lodged in his throat and how the doctor finally had to remove it after his father had eaten a whole loaf of bread trying to dislodge it. His father, Martone's mother said, kept it taped to the inside of his wallet, a milky hair-thin sliver. To this day Martone always eats fish with soft rolls. He takes a bite of bread after every bite of fish, even if it is said to be a fillet. In the hospital, the operation did not go as planned. Or more precisely, the operation went well until after it was over. Martone remembers nothing of the procedure and did not recognize the odor of the anesthetic to be anything like that of the chemicals in fingernail polish remover. He recalls the doctor asking him to count backwards even though his mouth was covered by the mask and then a sound like the sawing of cicadas on a summer evening. His mother loves to tell the story of what happened in the recovery room after the surgery. The hemorrhaging of blood from Martone's nose and mouth. His mother running out of the room and down the hall screaming. A nurse calmly walking her back down the corridor, explaining that this is normal, a little blood, nothing to worry about, she says, patting Martone's mother's hand. Until the nurse sees the blood welling out of the patient, who is coughing and sputtering in his sleep, drowning, Martone's mother says later, in his own blood. The sheet, Martone's mother always says, was completely soaked red. Flinging off Martone's mother, the nurse rushes the gurney away and disappears back into the operating suite. But it all worked out in the end. Martone's hospital stay stretched out to days, long enough that the diet of Popsicles, ice cream, and gelatin became monotonous and unappealing. His doctors and nurses and his mother remained vague as to why his overnight stay, the one for which he so rigorously prepared, extended to a week. Martone remembers his mother in his hospital room, reading to him from his favorite book, one that he had fortunately packed for his visit, *Mike Mulligan and His Steam Shovel*. Its graphic charcoal images of the steam shovel racing to scoop out the cellar of the town hall before sundown took on a new urgency during his recovery. It was not until years later that Martone's mother finally told Martone of the recovery room, the nurse, and the sheets soaked with blood. Recently, during a visit home after telling that story again, Martone's mother had her son look into her own mouth. Martone (who since childhood has suffered from an overactive vagus nerve, which causes him to get lightheaded and fainty, a white coat hypertension, when confronted with most things medical) looked quickly into his mother's open mouth, back to her throat, a throat that still contained its tonsils. He had not really seen much of anything but his mother's plump tongue, her tangle of teeth, and the converging lines of sight leading to the opening of her dark throat. "What am I looking at?" he asked her. She told him that she had two palatal tori—bulges or rounded projections, bony swellings on the roof of her mouth. Martone wondered whether that was dangerous, life threatening. His mother assured him it was not. Martone could see that she was working her tongue over along the new ridges of her palate. But then she said, "Of course, you never know."

CONTRIBUTOR'S NOTE

Michael Martone was born in Fort Wayne, Indiana. He attended Indiana University in Bloomington, where he lived in Brown Hall, one dorm in a quadrangle of buildings each named for nearby counties—Brown, Greene, Monroe, Morgan. His dorm was part of the Living Learning Center, which operated as a small, more intimate college within the much larger, anonymous university. At the Living Learning Center the self-motivated and ambitious students that the program attracted put on plays, published their own newspaper and literary magazine, and maintained a darkroom and an art gallery. Weekly, the students held poetry readings in the coffee house they converted from the old television lounge. A future governor of the state of Indiana, who later became a United States senator mentioned frequently as a vice-presidential candidate, lived right down the hall from Martone. Martone lived with the sons and daughters of university professors and lawyers and doctors, but the dorm also housed a contingent of varsity swimmers, just as obsessive as their nonathletic neighbors. The swimmers were part of the famous team coached by Doc Councilman. The pool was nearby, arguing for the billeting of its users in the Living Learning Center. Martone would be awakened very early when a pod of swimmers banged down the hallway and stairwell on the way to train. Next door, Martone's neighbor, who played on his record player, constantly and too loud, Gordon Lightfoot singing "The Wreck of the Edmund Fitzgerald," was washed up at eighteen years old as a competitive swimmer. He had taken up intercollegiate water polo to remain eligible for his scholarship as his splits for the individual medley had fallen off. Martone knew that he still shaved down, trying through the ritual to coax a few more tenths of seconds from his hairless body. Also on Martone's floor was Jack Donahue, who would become an assistant secretary of labor during the first Clinton administration. One evening Jack invited Martone to his political science class being held in the dorm's coffee house. The teacher was conducting an educational game that simulated, Jack said, the dynamics of world politics and international economic systems. The class was small and needed bodies for the simulation to work. Martone, who wasn't doing anything but listening to "The Wreck of the Edmund Fitzgerald," was quite happy to participate. Once in place, Martone was assigned a role of a small, poor African republic recently liberated from a colonial past. The professor had actually dealt out cards to all the students and their dragooned volunteers to see who would be what nation-state. Most of them were small, poor countries, though some were large, poor countries. Only a few got to be countries like the United States or Germany or Japan or France or Great Britain. Those countries got to draw cards from a special deck while Martone and the rest received cards from a deck dealt by the professor. The cards the players received contained information pertinent to their nations for the year the hand represented. Martone learned of his country's booming population, its declining food production, its outbreak of disease, and a minor guerilla incursion on its border. The numbers indicated that famine was imminent, disaster on the horizon. After all the participants assessed the cards they had been dealt, the game called for a period of negotiation among its players. The poor countries appealed to the rich ones for assistance—aid of some metric tons of surplus food or advisers to train their struggling militias. At first the players who held the rich countries were generous with their wealth, but as further hands were dealt and the demands upon their largesse increased they became more cautious, demanding more natural resources or labor from those countries who asked, round after round, for more assistance. That was the point of the game, of course, for the students who controlled the wealth to discover how easily they became greedy, indifferent, and callous even when nothing really was at stake but these abstractions. Martone dreaded approaching the student who held all the cards during the diplomacy session. A significant percentage of Martone's population was now starving while it continued to multiply vigorously. His one liquid commodity of industrial diamonds had fallen into the hands of tribal warlords. First one and then another and another of the first-world countries had during their meetings asked him simply what was in this relationship for them. At last, after the next hand was dealt, Martone looked at his cards and realized that everyone in his country was dead or dying though babies were still being born. His country was a desert. Its forests had all been burned for fuel, its animals poached. Its polluted rivers were all diverted to neighboring countries for aborted power schemes. Its once abundant lakes were silted and brackish. The tribe that once lived on floating islands of reed, making distinctive basketry from the same versatile fiber, was now scattered or emigrated to Europe to work as taxi drivers or street vendors. Martone turned the cards back over on his desk. And during the negotiation session, as the participants milled about the room seeking audiences and making deals with each other, Martone went out for a drink of real water, deciding as he drank that he wouldn't go back in for another round. Instead he walked out onto the quad at night and made his way over to the pool, where he watched his dormmate play water polo. The bobbing rubber-capped heads of the players looked like balls floating on the surface of the water. Then the ball that was actually a ball and not another bobbing head would go sailing down the pool, the floating heads below turning slowly in the water to watch it go by. "Lake Superior, it is said, never gives up her dead," Martone thought as he watched. It was days later in the cafeteria at lunch that Jack Donahue sought out Martone to tell him how impressed his professor had been with the way Martone had played the game. This surprised Martone, since from his perspective he had captained his country to a devastating end. But an interesting thing had happened that night, Donahue told him. Several rounds of the game, perhaps as many as five or six turns of hands being dealt and negotiations conducted, had been played before anyone noticed Martone's absence. Then the scattered pile of cards he had left behind was discovered, and the narrative of his country's decay and doom was archaeologically reconstructed from its relics. This, then, had been the lesson all along, this dwindling and disappearance. No one had even noticed as a whole nation vanished. That's what happens in the real world, the professor had said. It hadn't been a simulation at all. This appearance of invisibility had been the whole point, and Martone hadn't been there to see it.

ABOUT THE AUTHOR

Michael Martone's current author's photograph was taken by Theresa Pappas, his wife, in the backyard of their house in Tuscaloosa, Alabama, in such a way that the steely trunk of the hackberry tree and the bushy leaves of the red-top shrubbery provide an interesting background to the subject's head shot. A thirty-six-exposure roll of Kodak Tri-X black and white was used. Halfway through the roll Martone changed his shirt from a blue and white vertical striped button-down long-sleeved-with-the-sleeves-rolled-up shirt to a black mock turtleneck long-sleeved tee. Martone retains the contact sheet and the negatives in an envelope from the developer from which he reprints the twenty-sixth exposure as the need arises, keeping it in a pile on his desk. The picture Martone used for his author photo before the current author photo described above shows Martone at his desk in his office in the attic of his house in Syracuse, New York. There were actually two pictures taken that day and in that place by Nick

Lisi, a local newspaper photographer, who took a roll of color shots for an article that ran in the *Post-Standard*, and Martone has used both of them on occasion. One looks down upon Martone looking up, his elbows on the messy desk, his fist on his cheeks. The other is taken from floor level looking up at Martone sitting before his littered desk. His legs are crossed and he is wearing a pair of white-on-black Converse Chuck Taylor low-cut basketball shoes. If you look carefully, you can see an unresolved checking statement, an advertisement for a book by Toni Morrison that has her author's photograph, and an annual statement for Ben and Jerry's Ice Cream company, along with the detritus of pens, paper clips, pencils, envelopes, floppy disks, coasters, and indistinguishable business and index cards. Martone had twenty-five shares of Ben and Jerry's Ice Cream until he was forced to sell when the company was purchased by Unilever, which resulted in a profit for Martone of $1,562.34. These pictures are significant in that they are the only official author photographs where Martone, the subject, is wearing his glasses. Somewhere on the desk is a folder with several prints of the author photo Martone was using at the time these new author photos were being taken. That author photo had been taken three years before and showed Martone standing in the middle of Massachusetts Avenue in Harvard Square wearing a barn coat, very baggy pants, and black and white saddle shoes. Cars are passing on either side of Martone, who has his hands in his pockets. Martone cannot remember nor discover the photographer's name and hopes, on the outside chance that he reads this, that he will get back in touch with Martone. But Martone does remember talking with the photographer as he loaded up his camera, a Hasselblad, double reflex, about his adopted son. He also told Martone how the camera was made by hollowing out a solid cube of steel. The license tag on one of the passing cars can be read easily and was blurred out when the picture ran in a review in a short-lived local weekly tabloid. Martone, when he looks at that photograph, always thinks of the expression "short-lived." Martone's first author photo was the only one he has ever had taken by a photographer who specialized in taking author photographs. Kelly Wise took Martone's picture in Amherst, Massachusetts, before Martone was even an author. At the suggestion of Mark Kramer, who was a published author and whom Kelly Wise had come to Amherst, Massachusetts, to photograph, Kelly Wise photographed Martone as well. It had been fortunate that Martone was visiting Mark Kramer at the same time and that Mark Kramer told Kelly Wise that one day Martone would be an author and he would be ahead of the game. And that was what happened. When, a few years later, Martone needed an author's photo, he used the one taken in Mark Kramer's backyard that day. For some reason Martone has the eraser end of a pencil sticking out of his shirt pocket. Had he been expecting that he would be having his picture taken that day, Martone probably wouldn't have had the pencil in his pocket. The whole thing had been unexpected, and the picture retains a certain air of spontaneity. It is not exactly accurate that Martone has had only one photographer who specializes in photographs of authors take his picture. Jill Krementz took his picture, but it was not an author's photograph. At the time, Martone was escorting the author Kurt Vonnegut to the commencement ceremonies at Syracuse University, where he, Vonnegut, was to make an address, and Jill Krementz, who accompanied them, took several snapshots with an inexpensive camera. At the airport Martone, still wearing his academic hood, stands next to Kurt Vonnegut, still wearing his medieval soft velvet tasseled hat, in front of Martone's car. Jill Krementz sent that picture and several other informal shots, including one where Martone's eyes are closed, to Martone in a printed business envelope with the warning not to bend because there were photographs inside to document the occasion of Martone's short-lived role as host and guide.

CONTRIBUTOR'S NOTE

Michael Martone was born in Fort Wayne, Indiana, where he was known, in the womb, as Missy. At birth Michael Martone was named Michael Anthony Martone, the Anthony being his father's name and the name of his grandfather on his father's side. Names his parents called him, recorded in his extensive baby book (he was a firstborn), included Dolly, Peanut, and Bug. His grandfather on his mother's side called Martone Gigi-tone (the "g" is hard) all of his life. He was known as Tony's boy or as Patty's boy or as Junior's (Martone's father being known as Junior or simply June) or as Tony and Patty's boy. He was baptized at age six weeks as Michael or more exactly Michaelus, the Latin version of Michael. Though he was named Michael, Martone was soon being called Mickey by his parents and then by his grandparents and his aunts and uncles and cousins. As a child growing up in Fort Wayne, Indiana, which is also known as the Summit City, he assumed that he was named Mickey by his father after Mickey Mantle, the New

York Yankees baseball player, as a kind of homage to Mickey Mantle or a charm to aid Martone as he inaugurated his own Pee-Wee baseball career. It turned out that Martone's father—he told Martone when Martone asked—had named him Mickey after a good friend of his, Mickey Allen, who had lived across the street from Martone's father's boyhood home on Brandriff Street and who had died when he, Mickey Allen, was fifteen. Martone's father had been a pallbearer at Mickey Allen's funeral, the first time Martone's father ever served in that capacity. In the summer, then, when playing Little League and later Pony and Colt League baseball, Martone was known as Mickey by his friends and teammates and by their parents and by the coaches and people who lived near the parks and watched the games. His family called Martone Mickey all the time, not just in the summer, but in school Martone was known as Michael because that was Martone's official name. It was shortened to Mike by his teachers, and Martone wrote "Mike" in the top right-hand corner of his papers all through school. To this day a few of Martone's classmates from fifth grade still call Martone not Mickey nor Mike but Monk when they see him. At all his high school reunions when he is called Monk by someone, Martone will be reminded of that afternoon years before when on the playground he imitated a monkey to endear himself to a group of kids and got called Monk for the first time. The name Monk began as a teasing joke but turned into a certified nickname after Martone drew a simple monkey character based on the Kilroy graffiti and then doodled a whole pantheon of Monk character variations from history, literature, and popular culture. General Monkarthur, Sir Monkalot, St. Francis of Monkssisi, the Monka Lisa, Monkinham Lincoln, Monkleberry Finn, Marilyn Monkroe, and even the Monkles, before the Monkees debuted. At the reunions the few men and women who remembered Martone as Monk don't remember why they remembered him as Monk, and every five years Martone reminds them of the story. Martone chose the name Joseph for a confirmation name after reading through lists of saints' names and their stories. At North Side High School almost everyone, except for those few still calling him Monk from elementary school or Mickey from summer baseball leagues, called him Mike. Martone discovered that Janine Burke liked him when in Mr. Humphrey's English class he, Mr. Humphrey, caught her writing Mrs. Michael Martone and Mrs. Janine Martone and Janine Martone on the inside cover of a notebook and made her read what she had written to the whole class. Mr. Lewinski, Martone's brilliant and very formal senior-year English teacher, called Martone Mr. Martone and did so even when, years later, Martone visited Mr. Lewinski, who was completely blind and slowly dying from diabetes in the hospital. When Martone graduated from high school, his diploma read "Michael Anthony Joseph Martone." All of those names were read by the vice principal, who was annoyed by the number of names and told Martone so during the commencement rehearsal. But Martone didn't know of any other time when he would ever use all of his names and submitted them again on the forms for his undergraduate and graduate diplomas. In college Martone belonged to the Mikes of America Club. For a nominal fee the club, based in Minneapolis, Minnesota, sent Martone a certificate and a quarterly newsletter. For years Martone, a member in good standing, carried a card he would produce at parties that said his name was Michael "Mike" Martone. In college and graduate school Martone would always answer "Michael" when a professor asked what he went by. He had thought of himself as a "Michael Martone," really, ever since Mr. Lewinski's class, in which he, the author of this note, first thought he might like to write and had thought about his nom de plume, his pen name, and practiced (as Janine Burke had done in another English class) a signature, his signature with the upward looping "h," "l," and "t." His family still calls him Mick but will force themselves to refer to him as Michael when speaking about him in third person to people who ask. For years now, since graduate school, where he met his wife, who always has called him simply Martone, Martone has thought of himself as Martone. Friends call Martone Martone, a strangely intimate construction in the way children in Tuscaloosa, Alabama, where Martone lives now with his wife, who still calls him Martone, call Martone Mr. Michael, that mix of formality and familiarity. Martone got married in a civil service at the Story County courthouse, in Nevada, Iowa. Along with his soon-to-be wife, Martone had to sign papers and register at the clerk's office before going into the courtroom. There was actually a big ancient book that both of them had to sign. Martone was not surprised to see that there were places that needed to be filled in labeled "Bride's Name before the Marriage" and "Bride's Name after the Marriage." His wife, who has several pet names that she calls Martone but refuses to let him share or use in public, kept her name. Martone was surprised to discover that there were also spaces that asked for "Groom's Name before Marriage" as well as "Groom's Name after Marriage." The possibility that there was this possibility of taking on a new name had never occurred to him. At that moment he couldn't think of what to call himself and simply signed Michael Martone twice. Martone and his soon-to-be wife and their two witnesses waited their turn in the courtroom, sitting in the jury box while the judge, who was going to conduct the service, sentenced someone to the county lockup. After the prisoner was led away the judge asked Martone whether there were rings and said he hadn't thought so when Martone said there weren't. Then he said, "Do you...," prompting the contributor named in this note to answer with an urgent head nod and a raising of his eyebrows, to fill in that blank he had left floating in the air with a name, any name.

126

CONTRIBUTOR'S NOTE

Michael Martone was born in Fort Wayne, Indiana. He attended graduate school in Baltimore at the Writing Seminars of the Johns Hopkins University, where the writer John Barth was his teacher. On the first day of class, John Barth suggested to his students that, since the degree program was only a year and since the semester-long seminar on which they were about to embark lent itself best to completed works, they should work exclusively in the short-story form under his tutelage. He also made it clear that he would read closely and critique thoroughly every story submitted to him and then confer extensively with the author about the work and about the comments on same from his or her fellow students. But, he went on, once his students graduated, he would no longer read their typescripts. Barth did go on to say that his students were welcome to send him offprints, galleys, and finished copies of magazines or books when they published new work, and he would read it all with relish and delight. In the twenty-five years since he graduated from Johns Hopkins, Martone has sent John Barth every one of the magazines and books in which any of his work has appeared. If this "Contributor's Note" is ever published, Martone will send one of the two complimentary copies he will receive from the editor (or if it is only one complimentary copy he will order an additional copy, usually at a discounted price) to his teacher who, probably in an unconscious moment of generosity, extended the invitation years ago to his students. Martone, after sending all of those magazines and books, always receives a brief, enthusiastic note of response from John Barth. During that first class John Barth also offered to give all of his students a reader's comment or "blurb" that each could use as each made his or her way in the world. Martone's "blurb" reads as follows:

> "Among our wealth of excellent new American short-story writers, Michael Martone is one particularly worth reading."

Martone has used the quotation, with deep appreciation, on each of his books—except the nonfiction ones, where it would not quite fit—and on all the accompanying promotional material. Perhaps because of the abiding affection and regard he holds for his teacher's gesture, Martone loves the genre of the "blurb" and is very happy to write one for anyone who asks. Just the other day, Martone received a copy of Susan Neville's book *The Invention of Flight*, published by the University of Georgia Press, as a token for the "blurb" Martone contributed to the book's back flap. It reads:

> "Among our wealth of excellent new American short-story writers, Susan Neville is one particularly worth reading."

Martone enjoys the discipline the form imposes to capture the essence of the work and something, too, of its author's style and voice. There is a lyrical compression to rendering a good "blurb." Martone has, several times, considered writing a book made up entirely of "blurbs" and has often made up "blurbs" for his own books, creating authors who are impressed mightily by his, Martone's, writing ability, his originality, his sensitivity, his utter readability, etc. John Barth, during the time Martone studied with him, concentrated on instilling in his students a thorough understanding of the formal construction of a story, employing the insights of narrative theorists to describe technically the workings of plot. Freytag's triangle (fig. 1), the famous upside-down checkmark, was utilized as a kind of can opener or crowbar to crack open a story.

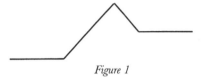

Figure 1

Martone took these lessons to heart and, years later in his own classes, routinely draws his students' attention to various parts of the story under consideration—its ground situation, vehicle, rising action, climax, and denouement. John Barth, in conference years ago, told Martone that what he, Martone, was writing were not technically stories. Martone said that he suspected that. What his teacher said exactly was: "This is not a story, technically." He was referring to something called "Fort Wayne Is Seventh on Hitler's List," a collage of thematic incidents that concerned scrapbooks, his grandfather, and airplanes. Martone understood how this wasn't a story. He had always had (and still does) a problem with the vehicle part of the formula, the story's "One day..." pivot that triggers the potential energy found in the story's ground situation. Martone has always been most interested in the ground situation. Martone's teacher went on to say that this was a descriptive distinction, and that his writing was up to something else. It was (and is) technically anecdotal, a series of interesting events, a rich tapestry of details. And, in the end, they settled on calling these things "fictions," a designation that has always seemed much more accurate. One day, a week before spring break, John Barth asked Martone whether he would, during the coming spring break, be interested in doing a little yard-work. Martone, being a long way from home and in need of some extra money for the typing of his thesis, took the job. In addition to pruning the shrubbery, picking up the felled deadwood branches from the winter, and raking the decaying leaves left over from the fall, Martone had to cut, trim, and apply fertilizer to the lawn. At the end of the week—its individual days memorable for the amazing sandwiches his teacher built for him each noon and for the forty minutes of conversation exchanged as the sandwiches were consumed—Martone worried about the consequences of his yard-work, especially the application of the fertilizer. John Barth had been working, when not preparing lunch, on reconciling the editorial queries attached to the galleys of his current massive novel and so did not oversee Martone's labor with the caustic chemical. A week later Martone walked up North Charles Street to inspect his work. His fears were realized. His mentor's lawn was striped brown and browner, the grass burned in a pattern that traced last week's progress back and forth, back and forth over it, a singed graph inscribed on the property. Martone stared at his handiwork. There was nothing to be done. Perhaps, Martone hoped, he won't notice. In any case, nothing, thankfully, was ever said about it. Of all the things that hadn't happened to Martone during his life to that point (both factual and fictional) in which, he believes, nothing much happens or is supposed to happen, this event was as much of such nothing as ever happened.

Or. Of all the things (both factual and fictional) that haven't happened to Martone during his life, this event was as much of nothing as he ever experienced.

Or. Of all the things (both factual and fictional) that haven't happened to Martone during his life, nothing more significant than this nothing has ever happened.

Or. Nothing more significant than this nothing hasn't ever happened.

CONTRIBUTOR'S NOTE

Michael Martone was born in Fort Wayne, Indiana, and grew up there on the city's north side in a new development called North Highlands. The subdivision's appellation was more or less accurate. Upon the relative flat river bottomland on which the city grew, its northern edge did encompass a slight rise in elevation, a matter of a couple dozen feet. That was enough of a difference to make North Highlands attractive to the builders of the city's television stations, who situated their studios and broadcast towers in that neighborhood. Fort Wayne was the last metropolitan market in the country to join the television networks, constructing the affiliates of NBC, CBS, and ABC late in 1959. Martone remembers being taken as a child up State Boulevard to the field where WKJG, the NBC property, was mounting its tower. Since Fort Wayne's citizens had nothing to watch yet on their new televisions, they went out to watch from a nearby but safe distance the progress being made on the new construction. The building of the first and tallest of the towers attracted huge crowds of people who watched for hours as the tubular lattice pieces were raised up and bolted into place. Martone was present and remembers the famous stunt the high ironworkers pulled on the gawkers below. He saw what appeared to be a body tumble from the top of the almost completed tower and plummet dramatically to the ground. The crowd was in shock and pressed toward the site of the accident only to discover the disfigured remains of a mannequin being mourned by a mocking ground crew. When the station at last went on the air it broadcast film of the diving body several times a day to fill the slots reserved for commercials not yet sold. Martone watched the body, a fuzzy shadow, cartwheel through the white sky. It looked as if the tumbling body made attempt after attempt to grab a rung on the tower paralleling its line of descent. People were filmed running to the point of impact. These were the first images he saw televised. Martone grew up in the shadows of the blinking towers, their guy wires arriving from above to be anchored into huge blocks of concrete parked in his neighbors' backyards. Martone made his first appearance on TV a few years later. Having entered and won a contest one autumn, writing an essay extolling the virtues of apples (Johnny Appleseed is buried in Fort Wayne), Martone appeared with the winners from other age groups on a locally produced show airing near Halloween. It was then he discovered the technical methods used to tell stories on television. He was filmed with the other children trick-or-treating at a house near the station. Pretend you are trick-or-treating, they were told by Wayne Rothgeb, the show's host and the station's farm reporter. The lady who opened the door invited them all inside, where they had cookies. Later, when Martone watched himself on TV, he saw the group approaching the house, and when they disappeared through the door they appeared again in a kitchen and living room built inside the studio. Martone had been filmed there a few days before the trick-or-treating, he remembered. He read his essay, listened to the other children read their essays, and then they all bobbed for apples beneath blazing studio lights. He had wondered why they were told to wear costumes there, and now he understood. On the show the studio was the inside of the house they were going into even though the inside of the house they did go into was very different. It had been very dark, and no one read his or her essays there. Growing up near the television towers meant that Martone often took part in their productions, mainly as a member of the studio audiences of the children's after-school cartoon shows. There was a Bozo franchise show he went to several times, but the clown looked so different in color. Then there was Engineer John of *The Engineer John Show*, who came into Martone's home each afternoon piloting a big steam locomotive, hauling a cargo of old Looney Tunes and toys. Engineer John was John Seymour, an actual engineer at the station who had been pressed into service when they needed someone to introduce the cartoons. One whole year, Martone collected bottle caps from Pepsi bottles for a television show. The caps were to be the currency used in an on-air auction that another station produced. Hundreds of children crowded into the studio with their bags of bottle caps to bid on merchandise provided by area merchants. The local bottler sponsored the show, making the scavenging of their bottle caps a lucrative incentive to the marketing of their bottles. Martone felt fortunate that his grandfather was a loyal consumer of the product, drinking the cola with a few salted peanuts dropped in the bottom of the bottle. The filling station where he worked had a dispensing machine as well, and Martone retrieved the caps from it. In the end Martone had barely enough caps to even make an opening bid. Other children came to the studio wheeling garbage cans and cardboard dish barrels filled with the caps. Martone sat there silently, picking the cork lining out of the cap with his fingernail, while the bidding bounced around the studio. And a few months later, Martone was in the studio audience of another children's show showing cartoons. He got to sit behind a cardboard cutout of a character on the show, Quick Draw McGraw. Other kids also sat behind cardboard cutouts of Quick Draw McGraw. All were given school bells to ring when they recognized the character that the host, a man dressed as Quick Draw McGraw, was drawing. To Martone it looked like a duck. So he rang the bell and guessed that it was Donald Duck. It wasn't Donald Duck, so he rang again and asked whether it was Daffy Duck. The host continued to draw. It wasn't Daffy Duck either. The host continued to draw something that looked like a duck. Martone could not think of any other duck characters except the relatives of Donald Duck, so he tried all of them. Huey, Dewey, Louie, etc. Martone rang the school bell for each, and every time he was told he was incorrect. In the end the character the host was drawing was Pogo. A duck, Martone thought, he had never seen before. Martone was very disappointed that he hadn't guessed correctly, but that was also the show where he saw the first Yogi Bear cartoon ever broadcast. He watched it on the television in the television studio. Martone has been on television many times since those times in his childhood. When he is in Fort Wayne he sometimes talks a few minutes with Dick Florea, who does a public-service spot at noon. Martone tells Mr. Florea about his current book (they are always set in Fort Wayne). And now when he talks with his mother by phone she often says, "You were on TV again." She has seen her son on the public ac- cess channel, a tape of a reading he did at the Fort Wayne campus of Indiana University/Purdue University. Martone has found that they run the tape often. He likes thinking that his tiny tclcviscd im- age is so constantly projected into the homes of his hometown. He also likes to think about those various broadcast images of himself, here ringing a bell or here bobbing for apples, radiating outward from the planet since pretty near the inception of such radiation, a kind of immortality, he guesses. Martone remembers the lights of that evening on the campus and the lights of the other times he has been in front of a camera and how the lights that made it possible for him to be seen also made it impossible to see.

CONTRIBUTOR'S NOTE

Michael Martone was born in Fort Wayne, Indiana. After graduating from Indiana University and before enrolling at the Johns Hopkins University, Martone worked as a night auditor at the Fort Wayne Marriott. He had hoped his responsibilities in the position would be minimal given the hours, eleven o'clock at night to seven the next morning. He thought that after checking in a few late arrivals he would be able to work on his writing. He had recently published his first short story, "Story Problems," in a magazine published in Macomb, Illinois, called *Mississippi Valley Review*, and he felt he was on the right track. But the job of the night auditor was much too complicated, he learned, and the night shift, in its way, the busiest one by far. So Martone ended up not writing a thing and remembers being tired all the time because he could never get his internal clock reset to the late hours. He ate supper for breakfast and fitfully napped during the daylight. He worked with two other auditors, Pete and Dave, who had grown accustomed to the shift, having done the job for a decade each. Pete and Dave tutored Martone in all the arcane math and mechanical posting, the duties of the night auditor. They also teased him, an initiation of sorts into the more bizarre aspects of the position. For example, if the front desk (Martone's station) were ever to be robbed in the middle of the night, Pete and Dave told him, the thief would have to kill you. They explained that the driveway was too far from the highway, giving the recently robbed plenty of time to call the police before the robber had even cleared the parking lot. Perhaps, Martone suggested, he would tie us up. Why bother, Pete and Dave replied, when there is a much more efficient way to proceed. The same distance from the highway would also guarantee that no one would notice a murder being committed at the hotel while they were just passing by. Martone was on duty the night Vernon Jordan was shot on the front steps of the hotel. Martone had heard the crack of what he realized later was the rifle's report. He leaped over the desk and ran through the revolving door to see the crumpled pile of a man on the ground being tended to by his hysterical companion. The night was dark and quiet save for the ambient whoosh of the cars on the distant interstate where, it turned out, the assassin had fired from the overpass. Vernon Jordan, who at the time was the director of the National Urban League and later advised President Clinton, survived. Martone called the police and brought towels to help staunch the bleeding. Vernon Jordan, in town to give a speech, had been stalked across the country by his assailant, who finally decided that this would be the opportune moment to kill him at last. He was two hundred yards away. The lights of the hotel lobby behind Vernon Jordan cast him into an easily acquired silhouette. After a few days the furor died down, especially when it seemed Vernon Jordan would live, and he left for home and the assassin was caught fleeing the state. It all, finally, seemed like a dream, and Martone resumed his nightly fire walks through the hotel, stopping at each floor's utility room to check the pilot lights of the hot-water heaters. Pete and Dave had told him that there is nothing that makes a guest so angry as the absence of hot water in the morning. In the morning Martone would make the wake-up calls, ringing the rooms and greeting the sleepy guests fumbling with the phone. Occasionally the phone would ring and ring, go unanswered. The hotel had a policy that the guest had to be awakened if he or she had left a call. Often, the phone went unanswered because the guest was already in the shower or had left the property, leaving the bill to be charged on the already-run credit card. But policy dictated that the room be checked, and Pete and Dave never failed to remind Martone, whose task it was to investigate, that suicides always leave wake-up calls. Martone walked along the hallways of the hotel, all the doors numbered. He carried the pass-key on a huge ring, a ring large enough to wear around his neck in case he had to carry something, in case his hands had to be free. As night auditor, Martone was too busy to write, would not even begin to write a new story for several more months, not until he moved away from Fort Wayne, not until he arrived in Baltimore. He thought, what will happen when he finally leaves this hotel, this city? What will happen when he begins the story of his life as a writer? What will happen in the stories he will write? What will happen when he knocks on this door at the end of the hall, when he lets himself in with the passkey and announces that it is time to wake up? What will happen tomorrow? But then he remembered, standing at the door, it already was tomorrow, had been tomorrow since the time he reported for work.

CONTRIBUTOR'S NOTE

Michael Martone was born in Fort Wayne, Indiana. He currently teaches in the Program in Creative Writing at the University of Alabama. Prior to coming to Tuscaloosa, Martone taught writing and literature at Syracuse University. He drove out from Boston to look for a place to live and was shown by the realtor a house near the university where Raymond Carver had lived before he left the university. After his death Carver's wife, Tess Gallagher, had put the house on the market while still renting it to students. One of the selling points of the house, along with the forced-air furnace and the hardwood floors, was that this house had been Raymond Carver's house. Walking through the house, Martone asked the realtor whether this had been the house where Raymond Carver wrote "Cathedral" or if this had been the house in which the events depicted in the short story "Cathedral" had taken place or both. The realtor said she didn't know but would find out, if that was important. The fact that Raymond Carver had lived in the house and may or may not have written "Cathedral" there added about $20,000 to the asking price compared to similar houses in the neighborhood. Martone decided not to make a bid on Raymond Carver's house, buying instead a house a few blocks away, from an English professor moving to Ohio named Stephen Melville, who was, he told Martone, related to Herman, though that seemed to add little to the value of the house. It was while he was teaching at Syracuse that Martone, for the first and what he believes is the only time, ate gold. The gold he ate was in the form of decorative shavings sprinkled on the icing of a dark chocolate cake served at the end of a banquet whose purpose was to elicit a donation for the creative-writing program from an alumnus named Morton Janklow, a very successful lawyer and literary agent. Mr. Janklow, it was said by the people in the development office, was the first to employ an auction when selling a book to a publisher, soliciting many simultaneous bids that resulted in remarkably inflated advances for his many famous clients. Mr. Janklow had let it be known through his friend William Safire, the Nixon speechwriter and *New York Times* political columnist and lexicographer, that he, Mr. Janklow, might be interested in donating several million dollars to his alma mater. The people in development had targeted creative writing as the natural match for his largesse, since he agented writers and the program granted degrees to same, and so concocted an occasion for Mr. Janklow to "host" a party honoring an anniversary of the creative-writing program. The university would actually give the party, hoping that spending a small fortune would, in the end, attract a much larger one. The party would take place in New York City, at Lubin House, a property the university owned across from the Pierre Hotel, just off Fifth Avenue. Martone was told he would have to dress the part. He asked whether that meant a suit and was told by the people in development that it did. So he went to JCPenney's and bought a suit, a double-breasted wool blend in a subtle taupe houndstooth pattern. It was the first real suit he ever bought. Martone, in his new suit, standing in front of the mirror in Penney's while the salesman marked the sleeves and cuffs with soap, thought: John Gotti goes to college. This became his tag line whenever he wore the finished altered suit. He wore it to school to teach, thinking he might as well get some use out of it. "John Gotti goes to college," he said to his amused students. "John Gotti goes to college," he said to the women who worked in the office when he modeled it for them. "John Gotti goes to college," Martone said to people he met at the cocktail party before the dinner at the Lubin House. The people in development had invited other successful alumni who were writers or in publishing to the anniversary celebration, hoping that they too would get into the spirit of giving demonstrated by Morton Janklow. Steve Croft, the *60 Minutes* correspondent, was there. Jay McInerney, who had written the novel *Bright Lights, Big City*, was there. And Martone thinks Joyce Carol Oates was there too, though that might have been another dinner. But Gay Talese was there for sure, as was Ken Auletta, who was writing for the *New Yorker* and who brought his wife, Amanda "Binky" Urban, another famous literary agent. When introduced, Martone did not repeat to Mr. Talese or Mr. Auletta his ice-breaking observation that he, Martone, might look like John Gotti in a college setting, and the name John Gotti, who was at the time under indictment in New York City, where the party was being held, did not come up. At the open bar where Martone asked for a Coke, he kidded the bartender, suggesting that he, the bartender, wasn't really a bartender, was probably an actor moonlighting, waiting for a break. The bartender didn't take offense, saying he wasn't an aspiring actor but aspired to be like some people in the room. "That's Jay McInerney," the bartender indicated to Martone. "Do you know who he is?" he asked Martone. When Martone, pretending, said he didn't know, the bartender said, "Perhaps the greatest writer of his generation." Martone wondered who the bartender thought he, Martone, was, but then remembered his new suit that did perhaps not make him look like a mobster but did disguise him enough so that he could not be seen as a writer. Martone had invited his agent, Sallie Gouverneur, who could only come for the dinner. While they all ate the cake with the real gold frosting, Mr. Janklow made a speech and toasted the creative-writing program at Syracuse University. Martone at one time had a girlfriend, Karen K. Potts, who told him that humans accumulated gold salts in a particular place in the body in the same way iodine found its way to the thyroid gland and radium settled in the teeth and bones. Gold, she said, collected in the brain, in the thalamus, where sensory impulses are relayed to the cerebral cortex. "The seat of emotion," she called it. Martone thought of that as he ate the pure gold shavings. He had eaten the cake part of the cake first, saving the frosting and its gold dust for last. Martone was a bit drunk from the champagne but could not, no matter how hard he concentrated, taste the gold, coated as it was with the paste of cocoa and sugar and butter. The faculty stayed that night at the mansion in the city. Martone went to sleep after playing a game of eight ball with his colleague Stephen Dobyns. He made sure to neatly pack his new suit into the cheap plastic garment bag that had come with it. At the same time, Mary Karr and Tobias Wolff went across the street with Toby's agent Amanda "Binky" Urban, and Mary pitched a book that would become *The Liars' Club* in a bar in the Pierre Hotel. And four weeks later the chancellor of the university, a man named Shaw, who was from Wisconsin, Martone thinks, met Mr. Janklow for lunch at the Four Seasons restaurant and made what the people in development call "the Ask," asking Mr. Janklow over soup for millions of dollars for the program in creative writing and was told, while they waited for their main courses of raw beef, that he, Mr. Janklow, had decided to give the money to Columbia, his law school, instead. After that, they finished their meal together, talking about the university when Mr. Janklow and Mr. Safire had been students there and about the current lacrosse team. They even had dessert before departing amiably outside the Seagram Building.

VITA

Michael Martone was born in Fort Wayne, Indiana, and worked his entire adult life fifty miles from there in Warsaw, Indiana, for the Biomet Corporation, a manufacturer of orthopedic prosthetic appliances and diagnostic and therapeutic devices, as an in-house copywriter and advertising consultant. He was also active in the local Wagon Wheel Dinner Theater, where he appeared in a dozen plays over the years, including leading roles in *Of Mice and Men*, *Flowers for Algernon*, and in a cameo role of Boo Radley in *To Kill a Mockingbird*. His works of fiction, collected in several resumes and vitae (including this one) as well as books, the last being *The Blue Guide to Indiana*, reflect the influence of his employer's products and the corporate culture he was a part of for over twenty-five years. The very brief fragments, paragraphs, and independent sections of his prose collages, often composed between appointments at his desk at Biomet, were continually recycled, renovated, and replaced in new renditions and subsequent editions.

Martone published a story entitled "Contributor's Note" in more than seventy journals, each time changing slightly the wording of a phrase, the consistency of tense, or redundancy of punctuation in order for each new piece to qualify as original and hence be eligible for further publication. His hobbies included sailing his hermaphrodite-rigged brig on nearby Winona Lake. His nautical interests along with his professional expertise led him to publish an influential pamphlet for the Department of Defense, detailing the construction and the eventual scrapping and salvaging of the U.S. Navy's first six frigates. The paper, used by the Navy in its attempt to sail, under its own power, the USS *Constitution* in Boston on 4 July 1999, demonstrated that a mere seven-foot section of the live oak keel and twenty-nine planks of the quarterdeck were original to the oldest commissioned warship in the world. Martone, who died in an equestrian accident at the age of forty-four, bequeathed his body, after his organs were harvested, to the gross anatomy lab at the Indiana University School of Medicine in Bloomington. His Mallory-head total hip device, his Bio-modular plastic shoulder joint assembly, his craniomaxillofacial rigid-fixation system, his titanium SpineLink modular spinal implant, his two aluminum Total Knees, and his seven stainless steel screws, all of the above employing Biomet's patented and proprietary porous plasma-spray coating technology and ArCom polyethylene manufacturing process, were recovered during Martone's dissection and are now on display in the lobby of the Biomet corporate headquarters.

CONTRIBUTOR'S NOTE

Michael Martone was born in Fort Wayne, Indiana, where at the age of nineteen years, four months, three days, twenty-two minutes, and an indeterminate number of seconds old he experienced, for the first time, human sexual intercourse. By human sexual intercourse, Martone means that he placed his erect penis inside a woman's vagina, where it remained until Martone ejaculated seminal fluid. This took place in the part of Fort Wayne, Indiana, that was the living room floor of his parents' house at 8222 Northwood Park Drive. The woman whose vagina Martone's erect penis remained inside of until ejaculation has a name but won't be named here because Martone, who remembers her name clearly, hasn't asked her whether he could use her name in this context, even though he is still occasionally in touch via e-mail with her at her home in Noblesville, Indiana. This was not the first time that Martone's erect penis had been placed inside a woman's vagina. That took place in a dorm room at Ball State University. Martone is not in contact with the woman whose vagina that was, and in any case no ejaculation occurred while his penis was there. Nor was this the first time an ejaculation occurred. That happened in a bathtub in Fort Wayne, Indiana, when Martone was almost twelve years old and is recounted, in a fictional guise, in one of the stories in his book *Pensées: The Thoughts of Dan Quayle*, in which the character of Dan Quayle remembers the first time he ejaculates. On the night in question, on the floor of the living room in Martone's parents' house, Martone and his unnamed partner were clothed. So Martone had the sensation of actually inserting his erect penis through the opening created by the unzipped fly of his gray wool pants as well as the sensation of actually entering the vagina of his unnamed partner. She was wearing a dress and had slid off her underpants. She held them bunched in her right hand. Martone's parents were asleep in their bedroom down the hallway, or, if they were not asleep, did nothing to indicate that they were awake or even aware that their son and his date for that evening (a dinner at Win Schuler's restaurant down the road) were on the floor of their living room engaged in human sexual intercourse. It was their son's first occasion of the aforementioned activity though not the first occasion for his companion, who was, she assured Martone, "protected" and who had a serious and steady older boyfriend in law school in a different city. Martone would think of that evening often, and in the days and weeks that followed the event he took to taking naps on the floor on the spot where it had taken place. It was there, one day, when he awoke from such a nap that he found himself staring into the eyes of a brown squirrel that had somehow gotten into the living room, probably via the fireplace and its chimney. Martone and the squirrel both started. The latter sought refuge by climbing the drapes of the big picture window and running headlong into the clear panes of the sliding glass patio doors opposite the picture window. Martone tried to talk to the squirrel in order to calm down both the squirrel and himself while opening the patio doors, at last, and providing the squirrel with an avenue of escape. In the years following these events, Martone continued to have sexual intercourse with some other women. Unfortunately, Martone's circumstances were such as to necessitate that he still live with his parents in their house. The particulars then of these subsequent liaisons played out in details similar to the first, i.e., not usually in a bedroom but in some other part of the house as his parents slept or did not sleep. This situation might account for the number of occasions when Martone was caught by his mother while having human sexual intercourse. One such occasion occurred while Martone and Jane Doe (who is an attorney in a New England state and who did grant Martone permission to use her name in this contributor's note but not the name of the state where she currently lives) were on the kitchen floor when Martone's mother emerged from the bedroom because, she said, she smelled something burning. Once again Martone's mother caught Martone and Jane Doe in the back seat of the Pontiac Bonneville parked in the attached garage that the couple had utilized in order not to attract attention or alert Martone's mother to their activities as the earlier session on the kitchen floor had done. Martone and Jane Doe were again surprised by Martone's mother when she came home unexpectedly to close the windows of the house during a sustained and severe thunderstorm. She discovered her son, this time completely naked, with Jane Doe, also completely naked, in what, Martone pretty confidently believed, was the middle of human sexual intercourse as he defined it, in her, Martone's mother's, and her husband's queen-sized bed. In all of these cases where she had surprised her son, Martone's mother uttered something quickly, indicating that she too had been surprised, suggesting that her son and her son's friend should finish up or beg her pardon or, in the last instance, had better get dressed. As Martone began to dress, Jane Doe went to close the window, the window Martone's mother had wanted to close against the now pelting rain. Martone remembers to this day that Jane Doe, even though this was the third time they had been caught, blushed, the blush then dissipating as she went to the window, slid down the sash, and turned back to search for her clothes. Martone caught his own parents only once. He was in kindergarten, and it was a Saturday morning when he walked into his parent's bedroom to ask for breakfast. He found them wrapped up in each other and then wrapped up together in a tangle of sheets and blankets. "Toast, Mommy," was what he said, his mother said to him years later when they talked after his mother had caught him in the same bed with Jane Doe. Martone can understand why some memories reoccur with such clarity and intensity. The occasions in which he was interrupted by his mother while having human sexual intercourse with Jane Doe seem reasonable as bona fide memories worth retaining and revisiting as do the other times he had human sexual intercourse with Jane Doe and was not surprised by his mother's intervention. But he does not remember, really, the moment he walked in on his parents and asked for toast to be made by his mother. Perhaps at that moment he could make no sense of what he was seeing. The event was planted there by his mother years later when she told him of the time he walked in on his parents and asked for toast. And all of this, all of the above, occurred to Martone only after he arrived early at the Doe and Doe Funeral Home (an establishment where, coincidentally, Jane Doe's father worked as a funeral director until his death) and caught an employee furtively applying rouge to his mother's bloodless cheek as she lay in her casket in preparation for her public showing and wake later that evening.

CONTRIBUTOR'S NOTE

Michael Martone was born in Fort Wayne, Indiana. He is the author of several books of fiction and nonfiction, and in the course of publishing and promoting those books Martone has, upon occasion, given readings of his work at various venues including colleges and universities, bookstores, churches, and YMCAs. Martone's worst experience as a public reader of his own work happened at a YMCA in Cambridge, Massachusetts. Having given several readings by this point, Martone made sure, in a pre-reading ritual, that the pages of his manuscript were in order. It always irritated Martone (when he was in the audience for readings given by other writers) to witness the seemingly nervous habits of readers shuffling through their pages, searching for the right piece to begin with. Admittedly, this happened more often with poets, but the practice spurred Martone to always have his pages in order. So that night, right before he began his reading at the Y in Cambridge, Massachusetts, as he forced himself to yawn (an ancient platform-speaker's trick to relax the voice), Martone carefully not-ed the order of his pages by flipping though his manuscript, re-counting the numbers in the top right-hand corner. What made the evening such a disaster was that after reading, in order, the first eighteen pages of his story, Martone discovered, as he turned to the final page, that the final page was not there. Looking at the artificial wood-grain of the podium before him, Martone, cha-grined, announced that he seemed to be missing the final page and then summarized haltingly the missing information to a bemused and embarrassed audience. Since then Martone always checks to make sure that his pages are not only in order but all there. Over the years Martone has also had the occasion to organize and host reading series as well. He has found that, inevitably, the conversa-tion he has before the reading with his visiting writers turns to stories of other reading disasters and mishaps. Martone (while col-lecting these anecdotes in the hope of one day publishing an an-thology of readers' worst readings) noticed that one particular set of circumstances seemed to befall several poets. It concerned, with slight variations, the visiting poet showing up to read at a college or university only to discover his or her host taken ill or taking care of someone who is ill, excusing him or herself before the poet's intro-duction. The poet then is left in a room alone to discover only a few distracted people in the audience; often one of them is de-scribed as a homeless man and the remaining two or three as un-dergraduate students. The sparsity of the turnout added to the host's departure ratchets up the bleakness of the event. But, of course, it then gets even worse. The poet introduces himself or herself to the scant audience and reads his or her first poem, and then, in the patter that follows, suggests, since the crowd is so small, that it would be better if they just had an intimate conversation about poetry. The climax is always that one member of the audi-ence asks how long this is going to take because they, the students, are there in the unused room only to study. The homeless man (if he is in the story) then eats the stale snack crackers and chunks of dried-out cheese from the pitiful reception table. Martone has heard this story recounted by several poets as their worst reading experience. He realizes that it is either an extraordinary coincidence or a widely shared urban tale or anxious Jungian dream. Everyone agrees, however, that this is indeed the best of the worst reading stories, that it contains all the excruciating elements of fear and embarrassment inherent in this public occasion for participants who are, by nature, shy of public occasions. When it comes to readings, Martone thinks often of water. Water in a cup or bottle the only prop available to the platform reader beyond the pages of the manuscript and the occasion to futz with the microphone. Bottled water seems to be replacing the paper cup or glass tumbler. Bottles have eliminated the need for a pitcher, too, which only revealed the degree of nervousness in the tremor of pouring. A glass of water seems more refined than the now more prevalent plastic bottle. The construction of that vessel creates a dramatic gesture. The reader must tip the bottle up completely, one's lips affixed to the narrow opening, manipulating the glugging management of air and liquid, a pantomime of fellation. Martone, unscrewing the cap of the proffered bottle of water at his own readings, can't help but think of that as he tips his head back, the image feeding back to amplify his already active self-consciousness and embarrassment. Water, Martone thinks. As an organizer or host of various series of readings through his career, Martone has worried about water—the providing of it and its delivery devices. The task is made most difficult when there is more than one reader. Will the first reader drink out of both glasses, thereby "contaminating" the other reader's prepared and waiting glass? Martone has watched (admittedly with some horror) a reader hesitate when deciding which glass to take up, having forgotten where that reader had set down their drink after first imbibing. Martone has watched the looks of consternation cross the faces of readers in that position, gamely attempting to maintain informative patter between swallows. This confusion does not depend on an evening with two or more readers. Proprietary glasses can be confused simply between the reader and the person introducing the reader, who might have his or her own supply of water that is or isn't touched (introductions being relatively short in comparison to the readings themselves). Martone, when it is his role to introduce, usually remembers to take back to his seat his glass or bottle of water after the introduction, thereby leaving a clear, unambiguous field of play water-wise, as it were, for the introduced reader. Though this practice, the retrieval of the introducer's water by the introducer once the introduction has been made, creates an additional moment of awkwardness when the introducer and the introduce pass on the stage (one heading back to the seats and the other to the podium) during the obligatory polite applause-covered exchange between the introducer and the reader, the moment is already fraught. A handshake? A hug? A hug and kiss on the cheek? A high-five? It is the dramatized moment of appreciation for the introduction, a physical launch after the verbal one that has just ended. Martone, in the introductory role, complicates matters when his hands are full at that moment of contact with the notes of his introduction and now the water and its apparatus retrieved to avoid the future confusion of the speaker. Few readers ever finish all of their water during their reading. They are good at rationing it out over the course of the evening's performance, not wanting to be caught short during the crucial crescendo moments of the delivery. Martone knows that there is nothing worse than dry mouth (both the syndrome and the symptom). In his role as host of a reading, he is often faced with what to do with the leftover water of his guests who are (after greeting his or her enthusiastic listeners before the stage, signing some books and shaking hands) taking off to the evening's reception. Martone is left behind to secure the room, coil the microphone cables, clean up, kill the lights. Part of the cleaning up part has always included the disposing of the evening's water. Often the lecture halls and auditoriums are not outfitted with a sink. Indeed, the whole point of the headache of providing water in the first place has been the fact that the hall is not in close proximity to sources of water. So Martone has found that he has fallen into the habit of finishing the water himself, drinking the dregs from the glasses or bottles left by the readers like a priest ingesting the leftover Eucharist at the end of Mass. Martone does this more out of a sense of neatness and order, but, he supposes, there is some of the spirit involved as well. He has witnessed some really amazing performances, listened to the work of famous and remarkably gifted writers. And he has drunk their leftover water. Perhaps a part of him believes some of that talent and skill will find its way into his own metabolism through this communion with greatness. It is a kind of inoculation, by means of this tainted fluid, with the cooties of the greatest. Martone hopes, as he drinks, that its inspirational properties, if not the medicinal ones, have "taken."

Contributor's Note

Michael Martone was born in Fort Wayne, Indiana, in 1955. In 1999, as Martone awoke one morning from uneasy dreams, he found himself transformed into a gigantic insect. He was lying on his hard, as it were armor-plated, back, and when he lifted his head a little he could see his domelike brown belly divided into stiff arched segments on top of which the bed quilt could hardly stay put and was about to slide off completely. His numerous legs, which were pitifully thin compared to the rest of his bulk, waved helplessly before his eyes. This extraordinary metamorphosis occurred during the run-up to the universal celebration of the approaching millennium. His mother and her good friend Irene Walters had been appointed by the mayor of Fort Wayne to plan and execute a series of cultural events and commemorations culminating in a massive downtown fireworks display on this special New Year's Eve. Martone's mother and Irene Walters had worked together a few years before this, organizing the city's celebration of its own bicentennial in 1994. Then, apple trees had been planted (Fort Wayne is the site of the grave of John Chapman, better known as Johnny Appleseed), park lands dedicated, time capsules unearthed and buried, statuary erected, parades launched, and epic historical pageants performed. Massive symbolic arches of welcome were constructed at all the land approaches to the city. Now the two women turned their attention and skill to the current chronological milestone. Included at every bicentennial event had been the unifying presence of General "Mad" Anthony Wayne, the city's namesake, who would appear mounted on a spirited hunter and in military uniform to welcome guests and participants, make announcements, award certificates, proclaim proclamations, issue orders, give directions, and bring things to a close, exhorting the participants to drive home safely. Martone had been General "Mad" Anthony Wayne, had once cut himself drawing the saber, and had developed an allergy to horses after the extended time spent that year with a horse. Then during the millennium celebration, Martone's mother and her friend and cochair Irene Walters decided, while having cocktails at the kitchen table in Martone's mother's house on Whitegate Drive, that these new festivities, too, needed a mascot, a costumed host, to mark each affair and venue as a certified event in the year-long series of events officially sanctioned and sponsored by the city of Fort Wayne—the now over two-hundred-year-old town where, in 1955, Michael Martone was born. They came up with the idea for a mascot. The mascot would be named Millie the Millipede, the common name for the crawling herbivorous myriapod of the class Diplopoda, punning cleverly with the occasion's designation of millennium. Martone's mother had always been fond of alliteration, and the fact that the consonance in this case had settled on the "m" sound pleased her enormously. They asked Martone, who at the time was using a spare bedroom in his mother's house to sleep and to write his first novel, which was set in Fort Wayne, Indiana, to once again don a uniform. Having nothing better to do and nervous about his precarious living arrangements in the house on Whitegate Drive, Martone agreed to be fitted for the prosthetic costume to simulate the scavenging bug representing the turn of a century as well as the turn of an entire millennium. The costume was quite lavish, mostly green shaped foam rubber and hard molded brown plastic creating a defined (what body builders call ripped) and rippling thorax. Coated with a soft green velveteen fur, the extended abdomen stretched a good ten feet behind Martone. The helmet mask fit snugly and was outfitted with reflecting compound eyes, serrated mandibles, and a curled proboscis reminiscent of a butterfly's. The antennae were numerous and hung braided in long dreadlocks down the back, which bristled with a mangy mane of cropped copper wire. Unlike "Mad" Anthony Wayne, Martone was not to speak when Millie the Millipede. Instead, he milled and waved, his many arms moving simultaneously, ingeniously linked to the actual veloured-gloved one that powered the locomotion of the rest. After the first few appearances the long train of the abdomen began to wear on the ground, the fabric abrading and the leaking stuffing leaving a trail behind. So Martone had to remember to gather up his rear end, draping it over his left, non-waving arm, tangled in with all the other left arms and legs. The costume scared the children it was meant to attract and entertain. It was hot and, after a while, steeped in Martone's sweat and could never be properly aired out or washed. Occasionally, while being introduced at festive gatherings in his role as official representative of the millennium committee, Martone worried about the name Millie and the projection of gender, wished wanly that the bug had been christened Milton or even Michael. After many weekends of many appearances, Martone would return to his room in his mother's house on Whitegate Drive and fall asleep still inside his battered costume. It was then, after one such exhausting weekend, that he awoke from uneasy dreams and found himself transformed into a gigantic insect. He was lying on his hard, as it were armor-plated, back, and when he lifted his head a little he could see his domelike brown belly divided into stiff arched segments on top of which the bed quilt could hardly stay put and was about to slide off completely. His numerous legs, which were pitifully thin compared to the rest of his bulk, waved helplessly before his eyes. It must have been his mother who tried to cover his bulk with the commemorative quilt she had commissioned during the bicentennial. She had liked to see him in his uniform during that celebration, adjusting his powdered wig and buttoning the buttons on his buff waistcoat before Martone left the house to drive to the stable for his horse. She had liked, too, the new costume and had had many pictures taken and framed with her son dressed as Millie the Millipede standing beside her, his (or her) many arms wrapped around her shoulders and waist and legs, the frayed abdomen tucked beneath the hem of Martone's mother's skirt as if constricting her legs. Martone's mother had always wanted to see the dawn of a new age, had thought long and carefully about the inventory of artifacts to be included in the soon-to-be buried time capsule. As cochair of the committee, she invoked her privilege to insert a copy of a small literary magazine that included a story written by her son about a man who became allergic to everything. The responsibilities of this second major civic initiative proved to be too much for Martone's mother, who died a few days before the fireworks display launched from downtown Fort Wayne's tallest building. During the Veterans Day parade, riding in an open car following Martone, who was dressed as Millie the Millipede and walking as the grand marshall, Martone's mother caught a cold from which she would never recover. She took to her bed, and as the days in the century dwindled, she entertained her son's reports of his most recent appearance as

Millie. He sat next to her in costume, though he had taken off his head. His mother said he looked as if he were being consumed by a worm. After he recounted the day's events Martone sat stroking his mother's hair and face with his good hand while the connected simulated arms or legs lamely stroked, like the oars of a boat, the sheets and blankets and quilts of her deathbed's bedclothes. The fireworks were fantastic, exploding above the city of Fort Wayne, Indiana. Martone's job that night was to hand out sparklers to any child, allowed to stay up late for this special occasion, who dared to take them from such a frightening creature.

CONTRIBUTOR'S NOTE

Michael Martone was born in Fort Wayne, Indiana, where he grew up and married, living with his high school sweetheart and first wife, Cindy née Caul, a hospital dietitian, and their dog, Debby, a boxer, on the near west side of the city in the former girlhood home of screen comedienne Carol Lombard, which they renovated by themselves to its Depression-era condition, converting it to a popular bed-and-breakfast. Martone attended the local regional campus, IPFW, where he majored in geology and business, meeting his second wife, the former Carol Clay, a loan officer in the university's financial office. They moved to nearby Grable, where Martone worked for May Sand and Stone as a gypsum board and sheetrock salesman, living in a remodeled congregational church with their two sons, Peter and Jay, and their cat, Rocky. Returning to Fort Wayne to work as a night auditor for the Marriott Hotel there, Martone met and married his next wife, Janine née Burke, who was an actuary and junior partner for the

Big Eight accounting firm Ernst & Ernst. She was, at the time they met, living during the workweek at the hotel while auditing the corporate books of the Rea Magnet Wire, headquartered in the city. The accounting team, dreading their week in the provincial backwater, delayed their arrival in Fort Wayne until late Sunday evening and left immediately from the factory on Friday to return to Chicago for the weekend. They would arrive after midnight during Martone's third shift, where he facilitated a speedy check-in by throwing their room keys at them as they entered the front door. Through her marriage to Martone and as a result of his enthusiastic promotion of Fort Wayne, his third wife eventually fell in love with her new hometown and remained there to raise their six children (including two sets of twins), tend her flock of ornamental bantam roosters, and open an H & R Block franchise after the couple separated and Martone left to attend graduate school in Baltimore. Moving with Martone from Fort Wayne to their new home in Charm City, Maryland, Patti Paine never wedded Martone, but the couple considered their relationship essentially a common-law marriage and lived, for all intents and purposes, as husband and wife in an apartment overlooking Love-Grove Alley on the city's near north side along with their daughter, Phoebe, from Patti's first marriage, and their not-approved-for-habitation pet, a fixed fisher mink named Norb. Patti always contended that she had been named Patti after Martone's mother, Patty, by her, Patti's, mother, who had been a classmate of Martone's mother, Patty, at North Side High School in Fort Wayne, Indiana, and for that reason Patti had always been Martone's mother's favorite wife among all of his wives. So their subsequent separation after Martone graduated from Johns Hopkins came as quite a blow to his mother, who never really recovered from the news. Martone, then teaching creative writing at a technical college in Ames, Iowa, met and married the former Sue Anne Schaffer Bakken Vermeer Nott

Potts Tadlock Doty, who at the time they met at the TIAA-Cref orientation session for new faculty hires was going by her maiden name, Smith. There they immediately used each other as beneficiaries on their generous life-insurance policies, provided by their state employer. They lived in a converted and, thus, nonworking Chicago and Northwestern Railway Pullman sleeper on a siding hard by the mainline of what is known as the Overland Route with their Great Dane, Scotty, and their Maine coon cat, Boo, until their divorce on grounds of irreconcilable differences on the anniversary of their benefits package. Martone then lived alone in an apartment above Frango's Cafe with cockatiel Barbie and a gecko with no name while he moonlighted from his job at the university as a corporate identity consultant for the new Barilla Pasta plant in nearby Huxley. Currently, Martone lives with his wife Nita and their three children, Primo, Secondo, and Maria Teresa, along with their cat, Chien, on the slopes of Vesuvius, near Martone's ancestral home in Italy, a town either destroyed in the war or by a volcanic eruption (depending on whom you talk to), where he is writing his memoir and participating, in a purely amateur way, as an archaeologist in a local Etruscan dig.

CONTRIBUTOR'S NOTE

Michael Martone was born in Fort Wayne, Indiana. In junior high school he became editor of the weekly student newspaper, called the *Franklin Post*. One of the first stories he published concerned the history of the name of the school, Franklin. Most everyone assumed that Franklin Junior High School had been named for Benjamin Franklin—one of the nation's founding fathers, inventor, printer, patriot, writer, ambassador to France. The name of the newspaper Martone edited was the *Post*, named after the *Saturday Evening Post*, a magazine purported to be started by Franklin, and the yearbook was called *The Kite and Key*, commemorating Franklin's experiments with electricity. There was a chipped plaster bust of Franklin perched on the window ledge of the stair landing, and in Mrs. Wiggs's ninth-grade English class students read *The Autobiography*. Martone, a ninth grader himself struggling with Franklin's *Autobiography*, began by doing an informative civics-minded feature introducing Franklinites (the paper's style-book designation for students of the school) to the interesting life of the junior high's namesake. Martone quickly discovered that the school had been named Franklin after Franklin Street, the street where Franklin Junior High School was located. Martone assumed naturally that Franklin Street had been named then for Benjamin Franklin and called the Fort Wayne Historical Society to confirm that. His research, however, revealed that the name was derived from someone else, a Franklin or Frank Hamilton, whose family had owned the land on which the school and the surrounding neighborhood had been situated. It had never occurred to Martone or to anyone else that Franklin had been someone's first name, though it made a little bit more sense when he thought of the neighborhood's other street names—Alice, Jesse, Edith. So Martone wrote an extensive article revealing the facts of the school's nomination and even conveyed a few particulars of Franklin Hamilton's life, though there wasn't much to report save that he was a member of the family that had donated the land to the city, including Hamilton Park, a block away, where the football team played their games. Mel Zehner, the assistant principal, was mildly upset that the mythic and very metaphorical connection of Ben Franklin to the school had been called into question. It would be too costly, he said, to change the names of the paper or the yearbook because of the name, let alone what this did to the idea of the school's traditions and continuity, and he suggested to Martone that he come to him before he ran any other similarly ambitious articles. Martone went back to publishing the various features he had inherited from previous editors, such as "Know the Ninth," a canned interview format consisting of a list of questions soliciting from the informants (members of the most senior class in the school) his or her likes but not dislikes. What is your favorite food? What is your favorite band? What is your favorite saying? What is your favorite day of the week? What is your favorite sport?

What is your favorite subject? What is your favorite holiday? What is your favorite season? What is your favorite color? Interestingly, the questions generated the same answers to the same questions year after year, the one variable being perhaps the favorite saying, but that often ran toward "What, me worry?" for the boys and "Groovy!" for the girls. Cheeseburgers had been the favorite food. The Beatles were the favorite band. Saturday, the day of the week. Basketball, the sport. Recess had been the joke response for the favorite subject. Or lunch. Or especially lunch on the day the cafeteria served cheeseburgers. Christmas and summer had been favorites. And blue the color for both boys and girls. Martone, as editor of the newspaper, self-administered the test and found, answering honestly, that he too favored cheeseburgers and summer and the Beatles and basketball and Saturday. When it came to color, his favorite was blue, and he thought about adding navy or powder or even Prussian to modify, slightly, his choice. He got Prussian from his current hobby that he would tell none of his classmates about, that of building and painting 54mm metal military miniatures, toy soldiers, at his basement workbench. He ended up using another color from his secret palette of uniform colors: buff. Just to be different. He did like the color of the tan that was used as the facing tint on the uniforms of American revolutionary soldiers. He thought then that in a little way this might make up for exposing the true namesake of the school, a way to be patriotic. Martone did not think when he affixed "buff" to the appropriate blank that the word also connoted nakedness. But the assistant principal, Mel Zehner, always reading the newspaper closely, brought it to his attention, and Martone was too embarrassed to explain the thinking that led him to the deviation. Today Martone's favorite food still is cheeseburgers. He finds that it is hard to top the Beatles. Basketball. Saturdays. Lunch. All have remained consistently his favorites. And if he is asked he would have to say that blue is his favorite color, pretty much any shade. The favorite saying has been less stable. For a while there he found he was saying "Ciao" a lot. "Righteous!" "Whatever floats your boat." "S'up?" "Knock yourself out." "Truly." The sound from the Bernard Herrmann theme from the movie *Psycho*. "Crash and burn." "Like being in a train wreck." "Say it don't spray it." And, perhaps, his current favorite, "Years pass. Time marches on."

CONTRIBUTOR'S NOTE

Michael Martone was born in Fort Wayne, Indiana. Martone has contributed a variety of freelance writing to many news and entertainment outlets, including the *New York Times Magazine*, National Public Radio, *Indianapolis Magazine*, the *Baltimore City Paper*, and the *Fort Wayne Journal-Gazette Rotogravure*, known as the *Local Roto*. He was a stringer for the UPI during the news agency's national election coverage in 1980 and a frequent correspondent to the independent newspapers *Nuvo* and *Breeze*, writing about places to travel to and about travel itself. Wearing his reporter's hat, Martone journeyed to Fairfield, Iowa, to investigate claims of human levitation at Maharishi International University and the possible health benefits of such a feat for a fitness magazine proposed by *Sports Illustrated* but that was, in the end, never launched. Martone arrived at the university and was ushered into an office to meet with deans, vice presidents, and the director of public relations. Lunch was ordered, and the representatives of the university, sensitive to skeptics, both the national media as well as their neighbors (the university buildings and grounds had recently been purchased from conservative and bankrupt Parsons College), seemed to overcompensate with a normalcy that bordered on parody by wearing blue blazers and cashmere cardigan sweaters and tartan vests with rep ties, khaki pants, and penny loafers. They urged Martone to eat the french fries ordered for lunch, insisting that they all ate french fries from time to time. A sociology professor handed out flip books for all to peruse while eating the french fries, demonstrating a marked decline in crime in cities where a certain percentage of its inhabitants practiced transcendental meditation. Graphs were produced displaying actuarial evidence of community health and lengthening mortality in the same populations with the corresponding depression of medical and rehabilitation costs. After lunch the chair of the physics department, a man who would later run for president as the candidate for TM's own political party, explained the physics of levitation by using both Newtonian and Einsteinian paradigms. He suggested, at the end of one very complicated equation scribbled on the board, that it was quite possible to fall up. Martone was then taken to one of the two domed meditation halls, the dome used by the men, to witness a demonstration of yogic hopping. Martone watched as a dozen men, their legs crossed in the lotus position, entered a very deep state of meditation. Then their legs began to twitch and shudder while their torsos remained relaxed, their eyes closed. And then they rose, in the same seated position, first a foot, then maybe two feet, vertically off the ground before landing back on the padded floor. His host told Martone that it got wild in here during the daily meditations, when hundreds of practitioners were hopping and falling all at once. He continued, saying it was all a matter of time before the critical mass of joint meditation would be met, thereby loosening the bonds of gravity altogether and allowing true hovering levitation if not sustained flight. These things would soon be achieved. Rumors in town were that they already were flying out in the domes, but Martone saw only the hopping going on in front of him. Hopping, his host assured him, was not being propelled by the physical exertion of the hopper but by a weakening in the gravitational field brought on by the power of meditation. Martone, sitting in an orange plastic chair on a stage where he was told the maharishi sat when he was in town, watched the men who were hopping below him. They flew up above the lip of the stage, their faces relaxed if not blissful. Later, Martone called his mother to tell her of his trip to Fairfield. His mother, up until the day she died, wrote occasional articles on the op-ed page of the *Fort Wayne News-Sentinel*, sentimental reports on the miracles of everyday life, catalogs of kindnesses she had witnessed that week, the ironic quirks that struck her fancy. She liked the idea that out above the cornfields of Iowa people were flying. But she was even more taken by the thought that just by thinking thoughts the world was changing for the better or, if not better, at least changed by the power of a thought. She wrote a piece about her son watching men levitate. What adventures her son has, she wrote. Martone thinks of his mother often. At one time he thought that if he could just think of all the possible ways a person could die he would be able, since death was always finally a surprise, to thwart death coming to pass. If he could have only held all those possible endings in mind, Martone thinks, the impossible might have been possible.

CONTRIBUTOR'S NOTE

Michael Martone was born in Fort Wayne, Indiana, in 1955. That same year, his mother was diagnosed with what is believed to be a terminal, congenital, bacterial, viral, genetic infection that has expressed itself symptomatically through a variety of neuromuscular, gastrointestinal, cardiovascular, endocrinological, skeletal, dermatological, pulmonary, hepatic-hemochramatical, urinary, and oncological dysfunction. The expression of this constellation of wasting pathogenic disorders in Martone's mother led to the identification of the syndrome with her chronic condition and resulted in the subsequent naming of the said condition as Martone's Mother's Disease a few months later by the National Institutes of Health. From a very early age Martone served as the poster boy in the role of the son whose mother had Martone's Mother's disease. During the initial fund-drives to combat and cure the disease, Martone helped found and has been associated with the Martone's Mother's Disease Society, serving on its board

179

of directors and being its spokeperson and unofficial chronicler and archivist. Martone oversees the sanctioned literature that emanates from the organization and has participated in the foundation of support groups, web sites, forums, publications, and research concerned with the condition. Martone even serves as host of the annual money-raising marathon broadcast by radio each Shrove Monday and Tuesday from Fort Wayne on station WOWO, 1190 AM. Every year for the last twenty-five years, Martone has made his way back home to the downtown studios of WOWO to inform the listening audience of northeastern Indiana, southeastern Michigan, and northwestern Ohio about the condition named for his mother's condition. At the same time, Martone solicits funds for therapeutic projects, environmental and population studies, and laboratory construction, sometimes garnering pledges totaling hundreds of dollars. For the marathons, Martone gathers a variety of local celebrities and entertainers who perform for Martone, who is answering the phones, and then sit down to talk with Martone on the air, recounting stories about their own mothers and their own mothers' conditions. Martone also interviews his father and his brother and other family members and friends, who all have stories to tell about his mother. In the wee hours of the morning, the studio temporarily empty save for a drowsy engineer, the phones are silent. Martone thinks of having a dinner break at Powers Hamburgers, open all night, up Harrison Street near the old Pennsylvania station. But it is then, in this darkest hour, that Martone turns to tell his own stories about his own mother, his lips a few inches from the microphone, his notes, scribbled during the intervening year, splayed on the table in front of him. He looks out the window where the world famous WOWO fire escape stands ready for escape in case there is a fire. Martone has watched his mother, he says, grow old, suffering from the vague pathology of her ills and afflictions. But, he says, he is still amazed

180

that she rouses herself each morning to contribute to the ongoing parade of anecdotes that people the world, anecdotes that, in sum, have been her life, a life, in spite of all its adversity and ever constant impending mortality, that has generated a wealth of viable memories. Martone says this into the microphone to a demographic that includes a few similarly afflicted and ill listeners and a couple of curious eavesdroppers out on the interstate who have just happened by while scanning the dial. That he is exhausted by this endless broadcast, that he gets confused from time to time about whether he is, as he always believed, recording his mother's death or whether, in fact, it was her life he has been recording all along, Martone no longer knows. His mother, one of the handful of listeners hearing this confession, perhaps the only listener hearing the confession, resolves right then and there to write a modest check, another modest check (along with a short note she'll pen right now), and send it to her son the first thing in the morning once she gets some sleep so she is ready to start another day.

CONTRIBUTOR'S NOTE

Michael Martone was born in Fort Wayne, Indiana. His first book of stories, *Alive and Dead in Indiana*, was published in the spring of 1984. He proofed the galleys for the book while he was in Greece, the summer of the year before its publication, with the poet Theresa Pappas, with whom he had been living for several years and whom he would marry around the time *Alive and Dead in Indiana* came out. They had allowed her relatives in Greece to believe that they were in fact married, which made it possible for them to share a room in an aunt's house in Athens but prompted further unsubtle questions from the family about the arrival of a first child. When asked, Martone and Pappas pantomimed for the landlords of the rooms they let, during their travels around the country and the islands, the crowns held above their heads, the climax of the Greek Orthodox wedding ceremony, signifying their marital status. Knowing that they would be in Greece for several months, they had their mail forwarded to the American Express office off Syntagma Square. Every time a bus or boat would bring them back to Athens and before they would depart for another part of the country, Martone would retrieve the accumulating letters and postcards while Pappas would sun in the square, fending off the patrolling local men looking to pick up the unaccompanied female tourist. It was on one such occasion that Martone received the expedited package containing the galleys of his book, the overlong stapled strips of paper folded once in the middle, the endless column of print scribbled and marked in red pencil. There were adhesive flags affixed to some pages alerting Martone to the copyeditor's queries and instructions on how to correct the proof and a letter about when and how to return it. Martone splurged and called his agent in New York, who surprised him by having arranged for Martone to borrow a house of another of her clients located on the island of Serifos. There, she said to Martone, he could complete the task of proofing his book away from the city and the solicitous relatives. She gave him an address in Athens where he could pick up the keys and directions to the house in the village on the island once he got there. Serifos is the third island in a chain of the western Cyclades between Kea and Kythnos and Sifnos and Milos. The house was in Chora, the village on the mountain that dominated the island. Their house and the other houses, churches, shops, dovecotes all painted bright white and trimmed in bright colors—blue, green, ochre—spilled down from the summit, where a couple of ancient windmills still turned. Their house was on an upper platea, a room and a loft with freshly painted red Dutch doors. Most of the other houses were deserted and the whole village quiet, they found out, since there was little water on the mountain. Most tourists and many of the islanders lived along the scalloped beach of the port below, where there was water and a few tavernas. Martone and Pappas hauled water from a well three tiers of steps and ramps away, using plastic gallon jugs they'd found in the house. Martone settled in to reread his stories about Indiana on Serifos, whose only story was that Perseus, wearing the winged sandals of Hermes, flew back to the island with the severed head of Medusa. The proof of that return were the eroding petrified figures of rock formations decorating the rugged ridge line on the higher mountain above the village. At night the Meltemi wind howled. It was late summer season. Martone read his book by kerosene lantern while his companion studied Greek or read again Patrick Leigh Fermor's book about the Mani, the war against the Turks, and the death of Byron. In the morning an old woman would open the top half of the front door and shout in at them, and they would try again with gestures and a little Greek to explain what they were doing in the little house in this mostly abandoned village. In the afternoon they walked the empty streets and alleys, taking abstract photographs of the angular walls and roofs cutting against the blue sky or the sheer walls of the mountain covered in green lichen. They watched from a terraced porch the tiny sailboats in the protected bay below attempt to round the point and head north toward Athens, only to stall there at the mouth of the harbor for hours, making little headway into the hot wind flowing south. Under these conditions Martone picked through the galleys, thinking then that his stories had to be made perfect, etched, as it were, in stone. He quarreled with many of the edits, writing elaborate justifications for his choice of words in the margins and as headnotes and footnotes. He read the stories backwards, word by word, to check for spelling, and the words read together this way made no sense, had become another language, were like the piles of rock found on the island. Every day Martone wrote postcards, writing to his correspondents about the water he and Pappas hauled, the piles of rock, the old woman who yelled each morning, the ruined dovecotes and derelict quarries. Soon, as he wrote, Martone forgot most of what he had written. He had forgotten, too, the stories he had written that he had only recently read again. He found he forgot not only the stories themselves but also all the recent marginalia that he had attached to the stories. Or more exactly, Martone could not remember the Martone who was the writer, who had written the stories and the queries, the postcards, and the letters back home, or where and under what conditions any of these things had been written. He had been lulled by the wind, the place, the island. He thought about all the places other than Indiana where he had written about Indiana. That story was, perhaps, done at a desk in a room in Baltimore; this one, maybe, finished in another room and another desk in Ames, Iowa; and this one composed on the porch of a beach house in Branford, Connecticut, on the Fourth of July, the smudge of fireworks on Long Island blooming just above the waters of the Sound. After a while, it didn't matter. Martone perched on a ledge above the harbor, watched for weeks as each morning the flotilla of boats struggled to round the point and escape the island only to run into the constant wall of wind. He returned, hauling a gallon of water to his borrowed house, where the poet Theresa Pappas was writing a poem about the island of Serifos. He went through the galleys of his first book, *Alive and Dead in Indiana*, and penciled "stet" next to all of his corrections of the corrections, even to the point of writing "stet" next to the stets the copyeditor had written when she, the copyeditor, had had her own second thoughts.

CONTRIBUTOR'S NOTE

Michael Martone was born in Fort Wayne, Indiana. His poems, stories, essays, and articles have appeared in over one hundred magazines and journals. When contributing to those periodicals Martone has also contributed a variety of contributor's notes solicited by the editors of the aforementioned magazines and journals at the time they accepted Martone's contribution. Most often, the request does not come with any instructions about how the note should be composed or what kind of information should be included. The editors simply ask, in their acceptance note, that Martone return the (signed) contract or permission form (if there is one) and perhaps also send a clean copy of the accepted submission or return a floppy disk to help in the typesetting of the work. The editors also include information on how to order additional copies and, sometimes, the chance to forward names and addresses of people who might order the magazine if they were to know that Martone's work was included, the latter being of special interest to Martone's mother. Martone always returns the form with her address so that the editors can send a notice and a chance to order the issue. "Don't forget to send a bio note" is usually all that is said about the contributor's note. Martone has noticed that even in the absence of any further instruction about what the contributor's note should be and what it should include, contributors' notes have settled into a conventional form. Notes most often include an indication of where the contributor was born or where he or she lives now, his or her most recently published poetry or prose, where he or she works or teaches or goes to school, and then ends with a more personal bit of information, such as a spouse's name or the number or names of children or pets. More rarely, the contributor will attempt a witty turn of phrase, a clever non sequitur in a seemingly spontaneous attempt to break the convention outlined above. These clever digressions always strike Martone as simply that—clever digressions—and it seems that feeling is shared by the majority of contributors who remain loyal to the understated and, one might say, elegant form that encapsulates a charming modesty and simple efficiency. Martone especially responds to that occasionally affixed sentence that comes at the end of some notes, indicating that this contributor's contribution is his or her first published piece. Martone finds that it adds a complex poignancy, a wistfulness, when (and if) he actually reads the contribution. Martone himself, in his first dozen contributor's notes, included the phrase, "This is his first published fiction." Martone has noticed that recently some editors have asked him to submit with his contributor's note a facsimile of his signature that is then reprinted near the standard biographical boilerplate in a kind of quasi-signed edition. The contributors' notes section becomes illustrated by the wide variety of cursive hands attached to the various contributors in a nostalgic, Martone supposes, allusion to the time when writers actually wrote by hand instead of typed. When asked to send a signature, Martone always becomes conscious of how little he writes anymore, his signatures degenerating, becoming vestigial. He does have two signatures, however. He uses one to sign checks and legal documents and the other to sign books when he has had occasion to sign his books for people who have asked that they be signed. And then there are editors who also ask their contributors to send a photograph, usually a photograph from childhood or at least not a current photograph in what Martone regards as a not so subtle satire of the traditional author's photograph. Martone has a picture, taken for his first communion, that he uses. He looks particularly angelic, since he had his first set of dental appliances installed a few days before the picture was taken, and his mouth ached from the procedure and the hardware. But all of this is to say that Martone has found the contributors' notes sections of magazines and journals often the most interesting part of the magazine or journal. He flips there first, usually in the back pages though sometimes in the front and even more rarely adjacent to the work itself either as a footnote or headnote. In a way it is like a party, Martone thinks, and when he receives his contributor's copy with his contribution and his contributor's note in its pages, Martone most often proceeds directly to the contributors' notes section to see who is attending the affair. Martone likes the feeling of being thrown together with these other writers and enjoys immensely reading about their lives. The party metaphor is really not accurate. It is more like a family of sympathetic souls partaking in the mysterious rituals of literary publishing. Any particular combination flares brightly for the moment, held together for the prescribed length of time by the periodical. Years later, Martone likes to look back at his old publications, especially the ones no longer in production. Reading through the contributors' notes of those long out of date publications is like convening a reunion of sorts—all the names, all the lives, all the words. Martone thinks of

Virgil Suarez as a brother, though he has never met Virgil Suarez anywhere save in the contributors' notes sections of magazines to which they had both contributed. Martone imagines other contributors doing what he does when the magazine appears, reading the contributors' notes section exclusively and contemplating these published tiny narratives of these characters called writers. It is a secret of his (though it is no longer a secret since it is mentioned here), this guilty pleasure. Martone published this contributor's note when he published a short fiction piece in *Rio Grande Review*, 21:1, in the spring of 2002. The contributor's note read:

> *Michael Martone is currently a professor of English at the University of Alabama, where he has been teaching since 1996. Before that he taught at Syracuse University, Iowa State University, and Harvard University. He lives with the poet Theresa Pappas and their two sons, Sam and Nick. Martone is the author of five books of fiction.*

David Kaczynski also contributed something to the same issue of the magazine. His contributor's note read:

> *David Kaczynski's work has appeared in* Writer's Forum *and* Sundial. *During the 1980s he lived in a rustic cabin in a remote desert area of west Texas. In 1996 he became the unwilling focus of media attention after the arrest of his brother, Theodore Kaczynski, the so-called Unabomber. He now lives in Schenectady, New York and is executive director of New Yorkers against the Death Penalty.*

For a while there, Martone shared space with David Kaczynski. Martone marvels at the intersections of lives, lines colliding and flying apart in the condensation of a cloud chamber window. Every word Martone sets down, finally, a choice that limits the universe, their trail across the page a fossil record of some life's life-story.